RETREAT

A DARK MENAGE ROMANCE

LOKI RENARD

1

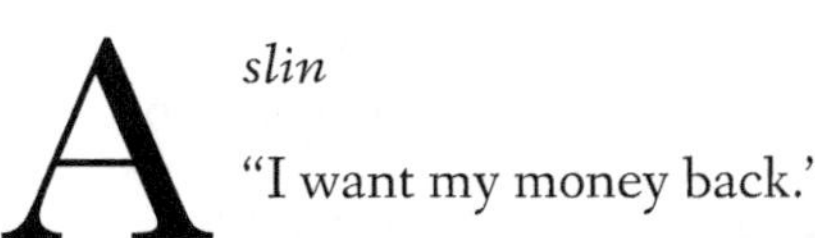

A*slin*

"I want my money back."

I'm staring at a monk. The word *monk* is wrong. They used it in the website, at least I thought they did. I assumed it meant chill old dude in a robe. This guy is no older than forty, muscled to hell and back, and hot when he's annoyed. I know that last part, because I've annoyed him, and that means I am getting the full benefit of his dark, aggressive stare. He's dripping slightly, but that's his fault.

See, I just got off a boat that I thought was taking me to a high-end retreat. What I discovered was nothing of the sort. There were just two guys on a rickety old bamboo dock, wearing camouflage pants and white vests. They grabbed my luggage out of the boat and before I knew it, the little motorboat had putted back down river. I was alone with two men I did not know, neither one of whom looked like he knew how to provide a hot stone massage.

"What the f... is going on here?" I inquired, gently. "Where's the retreat?"

"You're here," the blond said. "I'm Soren, and this is Jason."

"I don't see a cabana on the waterfront. I don't hear wind chimes. I don't smell incense. I don't have a complimentary margarita in my hand. This is false advertising."

"Brat," Jason growled under his breath.

That annoyed me. I didn't come all this way to be spoken down to. I came all this way for private pampering.

"I'm the customer," I reminded him. "I paid more than some people earn in a year to come here, so I better have a drink in my hand in the next thirty seconds, or I am going to..."

"ENOUGH!" Jason barked the word, his voice booming so loudly it scared the birds, and probably alligators, out of the water.

He yelled at me. I can't believe he yelled at me.

I did what any boss babe fourteen hours out from her last good cocktail, discovering herself deep in the wilds of a foreign land, and being yelled at by some jerk would do.

I pushed Jason into the water.

What would you have done?

Jason looks very attractive climbing back up onto the dock. I guess he didn't plan it, but he basically entered a wet t-shirt contest for me. The way the vest clings to his six-pack as he pulls himself up out of the water would make the internet explode if they could see it. I'm talking rippling muscles and perfect form. Holy...

He nails me with a dark, furious stare, but doesn't say anything to me. Instead he talks to the other guy.

"Get her up to camp, before I do something I'm going to regret."

"Oh. Nice. Threats of violence," I say as Soren takes me by the elbow, which is also a mistake. "I can't tell you what I'm going to do to your online reviews. I am going to make them look like..."

Soren, who is much taller than I am, bends down to put his lips by my ear. Unlike Jason, he doesn't yell. He speaks in a soft murmur that might actually be more intimidating.

"Little hint, Aslin," he says. "Behave yourself."

"What is that supposed to mean!?"

"It means you're obviously out of your depth, confused about what you've gotten yourself into, and in about as much trouble as you can be in. You've been here two minutes. So. Slow your roll. I know you can be a good girl when you want to be."

He punctuates his advice with a light pat to my ass. He barely taps me and immediately my entire body is flooded with mad endorphins.

But it's not the tap that gets me, and it's not the warning, purred in my ear. It's the way he looks at me. Not through me, but into me. I now know what it means to be penetrated by a stare. Most people think I'm a rich, spoiled pain in the rear. Soren's already seeing something else, talking directly to a part of me I keep hidden.

I am going to have to be very careful with this man. I didn't come here to be noticed. I came here to disappear.

That brings us to this moment. I am, apparently, in trouble. The 'house' such as it is, is more like a big gazebo. Very open to the elements at the sides, and basically no privacy whatsoever. I can't imagine where I'm supposed to... you know.

"Sit down," Jason says, pointing to the floor. There's nothing to sit on, of course. Not even a stupid little cushion thing. There's just a bamboo mat. Everything here is bamboo. The buildings are bamboo, the clothes are made of bamboo, the furniture is bamboo, and outside, the bamboo is also bamboo.

"Nope," I say.

Soren makes the argument moot by pressing on the backs of my knees and dropping me to the floor. I'm not used to being handled that casually and physically at the same time.

"What the fuck are you..."

He looks down at me with those icy blue eyes that belong in a cologne ad. "You came here to learn some discipline. Nothing's changed."

"Something has changed. My mind. I want to go home."

"You'll go home in ninety days, as agreed."

"Uh. No. I'll go home now." I start to get up. Being on my knees in front of this guy feels undignified and kind of filthy. I start to get up. That's a mistake.

CRACK!

There's a loud snapping sound. At first I don't connect it with anything in particular, and then a second later I feel a blazing hot line of pain right across the center of my ass.

"FUCK!" I scream at the top of my voice as I lunge forward, hands on my ass. That grip doesn't help. If anything it makes the pain worse. I roll over onto my back, while trying to keep my ass off the ground, which brings my knees up toward my chest, and my eyes up to the asshole who just hit me with a long piece of tapered bamboo. Unbe-fucking-lievable.

"You can't hit me! I paid for this!"

"Sure, I can," Soren says, his face relaxing into an easy grin. "You paid to be disciplined."

"No. I paid to learn how to be more at peace."

"Same thing," he says.

"It's fucking not. This feels more like one of those shows where they take some spoiled teen and make their lives miserable than the expensive, did I say, expensive as FUCK retreat I paid for."

"You're going to get what you paid for," Jason assures me.

"You're spoiled," Soren says. "And we won't spare the rod. Of course, if you do as you're told, there won't be any need for it. Now. Are you ready to settle in? Or do you need a little more orientation?"

This place is remote. I'm not even sure what country I am in anymore. On arrival, it felt like a place beyond borders and time. Now it feels like a place without human rights.

"I've changed my mind," I repeat.

"That's not an option. The boat won't return for three weeks with fresh supplies and walking out of here is not recommended without a guide. You've made a commitment to be here, to discover your true nature, and to find peace," Soren says.

"Yes. And nowhere did anything mention the big muscle-heads with the canes."

They look at each other, and I see the muscles in their jaws twitching. They're all but laughing at me. I'm not amused. I'm sore, I'm feeling very sorry for myself, and I need a fucking drink.

S*oren*

She's cute. She doesn't know it, but we almost didn't accept her application. Sass rolled off the essay portion thick as molasses, a particular sense of entitlement and even grandiosity. I'd put money down that she didn't read any of the terms and conditions. Too busy, too arrogant, to notice what she was signing up for.

Here's what I know about her. She's thirty-two years old, an executive, single, childless, career-driven, and absolutely riddled with anxiety she doesn't understand.

I convinced Jason she needed our help. And it's not like we're being swamped with people prepared to pay our fees. Nothing about this experience is cheap, but we promise it will be transformative.

Jason conceded I was probably right, then said she'd be more trouble than she was worth. I agreed with him. But we needed a challenge. I think we've gotten one.

Here we all are. Our guest is crouched on the ground, pouting up at me with those big brown eyes, looking at me like she doesn't know what to make of me. Her hair is messy from the pointless struggle she decided to engage in. Her jumpsuit is going to present a problem, because it is only a matter of time before I turn her over my knee, and when I do that, I like to have the recipient bare. The cane is a good tool for getting attention, or teaching a harsh lesson, but she needs a gentler introduction to having her ass spanked given how much of it she seems to need. She's not going to like it, but it's going to do her a world of good.

"I was tricked," she declares. "I thought this was going to be massages and mai tais on the beach. I thought it was cocktails on a cruise. I thought I'd be poolside with a pina colada in a coconut."

"How many different vacations did you think you'd booked, exactly?"

"Twenty grand worth of them," she snaps back at me. "Not this fucking primitive kink escape. You baited and switched me."

She wasn't tricked. If anything, she played herself. She's so spoiled. The kind of person for whom everything is someone else's fault.

It's actually astonishing how quickly the cane has ended up in my hand. I've never had to punish a client before. Most of them come here with some idea as to what to expect, and with a respect for Jason and me. Most of them want to change. They want to learn. They crave something different. I don't know what Aslin thought she'd get from this. I refuse to believe she booked the trip without knowing what it was. We have an essay portion for a reason. Aslin knows she needs this, or she wouldn't have applied. But that doesn't mean she wants it.

She's like a little girl, seeking out trouble because she knows she needs to feel what it is like to be in trouble. I can do that for her. I don't mind if she hates me. I'll be whatever she needs.

"Alright," Jason says, now that she seems to understand there might be consequences for her actions. "We're going to go over the rules of the retreat. This will save you further pain. Firstly, you do as you are told. We are in a remote region of Nepal, and there are real dangers here. Secondly, you do not leave this compound unattended, for much the same reason. Thirdly, you do as you're told."

A*slin*

What. The. Actual. Fuck. I can't believe what I'm hearing. I can't believe a sane person could form those words with a straight face. Do as I am told? They really don't know me at all. I've never done as I was told.

"Okay. You're both crazy, and I'm going home. I'll go sit by the dock."

Soren grips me by the back of my jumpsuit, fisting his hand in the loose fabric. "Not for at least three weeks, you're not," he says. "You paid us to provide a service, and we're going to provide it, whether you like it or not."

"But..."

"No buts," he says. "Settle down and do as you're told. Make this easier on yourself. Please."

"Please?"

"Yes, as in, please don't make me bend you over and cane you on your first day."

"You wouldn't!" I gasp, scandalized.

"I would," he says.

I look around again, as if there might be some additional cues besides the bamboo, which I am pretty sure is actually a plantation and not entirely native, but that's the least of my concerns right now. "What the... what is this place?"

Soren offers his hand to help me stand. I take it, only because I feel a little wobbly. I did know this was some kind of special retreat, but I chose it because how far it was from everything else. I didn't pay any attention to the details. They weren't important at the time.

"It's somewhere for people like you. People who can't get what they need anywhere else, in any other way. People who crave something nobody else seems to need, but they can't live without."

I look into his stunning blue eyes, and I feel like he might be the first person who has ever actually seen me. Most people just think I'm a bitch. They're not wrong.

"This is where you'll sleep, eat, and train," Soren says, indicating the gazebo. "Bathrooms are out back. Can't miss them. There's a rain shower too."

Of course the showers are cold. Of course they are. This is my personal bad place and I've manifested it by not paying attention while planning my escape from the real world. Fuck my actual life.

"I really can't do this," I say, turning around so I can face them both. "I mean, I made a huge mistake here. It's obvious we're all going to make each other crazy if I stay here, so why not just call the boat back — and don't tell me you can't, because there has to be some provision for emergencies."

"We're not using our emergency travel plans for you because you've thrown a tantrum on the first hour of the first day," Jason says grimly. This dude fucking hates me, I can already tell. Can't say I blame him. Most men learn to hate me sooner or later.

"This is the worst retreat ever. What am I even paying for? The accommodation is sub-par, the service is non-existent..."

"You're paying for our personal attention for the duration of your stay," Soren says. "And you're paying for Jason to keep his temper enough not to throw you in the river in return."

I look at Jason aghast. He does look like he thinks that would be a good idea.

"We're not going to hurt you..." Soren continues.

"Says the guy who hit me with a cane."

"That's different. That's what you're here for. You can't control your emotions or regulate your moods. Your chaos affects others, and it makes your life hard. You're isolated. And you're tired of it."

"I..." my jaw is fucking dropped. "I know I didn't write any of that on that ridiculously long form I had to fill in."

"You didn't have to," Soren says.

"Oh for fuck's sake..." I don't even know what I am swearing at. I just know that it feels good to swear. I'm still wearing my cute tropical style jumpsuit that actually worked on the boat, but when he talks to me like that, I feel naked. "Tell me I can get a drink, at least. Tell me you have beer."

"You can have a beer when you earn one," Jason says.

"Where do we sleep? There aren't even beds."

"There are bed rolls. They're stored away in the center pillar there, as is everything we need to cook and survive. We put them down every night, and we roll them away every morning. You'll do the same. Day begins at five in the morning. We meditate until seven, and..."

"Two hours! You expect me to stay awake for two hours at five in the morning? That's never going to happen."

"That's what the cane is supposed to be for. Keeping you focused if you need it. It's not supposed to be for teaching basic manners, but we can use it for that if you need it." Soren winks at me.

"Ugh! Fuck! I really don't want to do this anymore. I know I'm stuck here, but I'm not doing any of the meditation stuff. In fact, I'm not doing anything. I'll wait for the boat."

"You're going to get hungry down there at the dock," Jason says. His tone suggests it's a trump card, like he's going to be able to control me by rationing food.

"No," I say. "I won't."

"How do you figure? I'd bet good money those bags have a whole lot of designer clothes, maybe a few snacks, but no real rations."

"There's a river. I'll catch a fish."

Jason folds big, muscular wet arms over a big, muscular wet chest, casts a smug glance over at Soren, then back at me. Oh he thinks he's got me now.

"And what are you going to catch fish with?"

"I don't know. Maybe a fishing pole?"

He shakes his head. "We're not giving you a fishing pole."

And here it is. The most satisfying part of my vacation so far — and considering I already pushed this jerk into the river, that's saying a lot. These two have me pegged as some spoiled, useless brat from a distant city. And they're sort of right. But before that, I was a spoiled, useful brat from the country. I can fish. I can do other things, too.

I am enjoying myself immensely. I kneel down, open a pink shell case, and start assembling my rod. They're watching me, sort of stunned, like they've never seen a woman with a custom-built fishing rod before. I have a tackle box to match, naturally, and another little case with my emergency supplies. I had hoped to avoid dipping into them so soon but needs must.

2

S Jason and I watch as Aslin sets up a little pink camp stool right at the end of the dock, breaks out a little pink cocktail shaker, and proceeds to not only bait and cast her line, but make herself a bloody mary. This is supposed to be the first meditation of the retreat. We should be putting a stop to this, but hell if I'm not impressed.

"Looks like she can take care of herself," I muse.

"Told you she was more trouble than she was worth."

Jason's still annoyed about being pushed into the river. I don't think he's going to forgive her until he gets his hands on her. Good news is, that's not going to be long with the way she acts.

"She's feisty," I agree.

"You like her," he accuses me, brows drawing down over his eyes like he thinks I'm crazy.

"It won't help to not like her."

"I don't like her," he says. "Ten grand each is not enough to put up with that shit for twelve weeks. We undercharge for these things."

"Most people don't have twenty grand to spend on a vacation. Look on the bright side. She's going to keep you on your toes. You've gotten slow, Jase. Nobody would have been able to push you in a river a year ago. This will be good for both of us. We need a challenge as much as she needs to be taken care of."

He rubs his hands together. "I'll take care of her, alright."

A*slin*

"So. Where did you learn to fish?"

Soren is beside me, crouching next to me, a curious look on his handsome face. He has a faint growth of dirty blond beard hair coming through. Both of these men are very attractive. I suppose that helps when they charge the earth for their services. I imagine most women coming here probably fall down at their feet, drooling. I wonder how often these expensive vacations turn into remote fuckfests. Probably not that often, given how tense these guys are. There's some small part of me that wouldn't mind being at their feet, but it's not a part I intend on showing anybody ever.

"Fishing camp for ill-tempered spinsters," I say, without batting an eyelid.

"Uh huh. Don't like personal conversations?"

I'm starting to think I might actually like Jason more than Soren. I don't enjoy all this incisiveness. It makes me feel uneasy. Jason judged me unfairly and inaccurately as soon as he met me, and that's the kind of dunderheaded thinking I'm comfortable with.

"Where did you learn to lure women to the Nepalese forest? Is that like, a module in the military?"

"You weren't lured. You self-selected."

I sip my drink and watch the lure drift down the river. Yes. I did this to myself. As usual.

Jason comes stamping down the dock hard enough to frighten the fish.

"Get up here," he says. "It's time to mediate."

"I'm good. Thanks."

Jason has the absolute fucking nerve to grab me by the back of my cute jungle jumpsuit and pull me up off my stool. This man is clearly a very slow learner.

"You do what we tell you to do, when we tell you to do it, got it?" He snarls the words in my face.

I throw the remnants of my bloody mary into his face. Tomato juice and vodka are not great for the eyes. He drops me, cursing. I drop my rod on the dock, but I keep my glass and drain the last few dregs of it in triumph.

"That's it," Jason says, wiping his eyes with his shirt. "Strike one, two, and three all in one go."

He props his dirty boot up on the stool and throws me over his knee. The relative difference in our sizes means I am now dangling, my toes and the tips of my fingers similarly bereft of support. My hips are pressed over the hard, flexing line of his thigh in a contact that feels very intimate.

He slaps me. Hard. Hard enough to make tears instantly spring to my eyes — sort of like his eyes watered when I threw my drink in them, I guess.

"We have never had anybody who's made as much trouble as you have as quickly as you have," Jason lectures, as if that's not something I'm going to take immediate pride in. Tears in my eyes or not, I'm glad I'm making his life hard.

Every time he spanks me, I make a new vow of vengeance. He's not going to get away with this. I'm not sorry, and he can't make me sorry. They have basically kidnapped me at this point, even if I did pay twenty grand to have this experience.

His hand is big, and hard. His fingers curl around the outside of my cheeks, and every now and again, around the inside. I feel the tips of them grazing against the mercifully jumpsuit-clad but nevertheless extremely intimate parts of me. I don't think he means for me to enjoy this. I know he doesn't. He's trying to use pain and shame to make me sorry.

"You're a brat," he growls.

I expect him to tell me that I'm too old to behave this way. That's usually what unimpressed men throw in my face. They expect me to be tamed by now, for life to have shamed me into the submission shared by so many of my friends, a sort of gratitude to just be allowed to be around. I'm not ashamed of myself. I don't back down, and I'm not sorry. I'll never be sorry, no matter what he does.

This does fucking hurt, though. Every slap brings with it ache and heat and sting. I'm going to be feeling this long after he stops, which is precisely what he wants. He's a goddamn sadist. I know sadists like to see that they're inflicting pain. I'm not giving him the satisfaction. I am, however, giving him my most creative swears and curses.

I lose count of how many times he spanks me. Well over a dozen times. Maybe two dozen. His big, meaty, overgrown palm meets my ass over and over again.

Not all is lost, though. I still have the tiniest drops of my drink in my hand, and Soren has rescued my rod. That was nice of him. Mid-spank, I lick the glass. It has to help.

"Okay, that's enough of that." Jason sweeps the glass out of my fingers and hands it off to Soren. "You need to take this more seriously, or it's going to get a whole lot worse. There's a lot of bamboo here, girl."

I have no idea what that threat means. Maybe it's some kind of military thing. I don't get a lot of time to process whatever it was, anyway, because he's spanking me again, and harder this time, to make up for the few teaspoons of alcohol I got into my system.

"Ow! Christ! Okay! I'm sorry!"

That's what he wanted to hear, I guess, because he tips me up onto my feet and gives me a stern stare. He thinks he's made some kind of an impression. He has, but not the impression he thinks. My ass is stinging and sort of tingly. I feel excited and hot and sexy. He doesn't know this about me, but I love a fight. Even if I lose. Maybe even especially if I lose.

"You're an asshole, and I hate you."

My words just make him smirk. "Hate me all you like. Do as you're told."

"Nope. No. Not going to do that."

"Then get used to having a sore ass."

"And you can get used to having your ass sued, buddy."

"I'm not your buddy, girl."

"I'm not a girl. I'm a woman. With a lawyer on retainer. So. Just you wait."

"I will wait. Wait for someone to bother coming out here to serve me a lawsuit for spanking your ass."

He's probably right, but that's not going to stop me from threatening him. Threats are pretty much all I've got.

"Put your bags in your cabin and come sit for meditation," he says, as if nothing fucked up has just happened. As if they thrash a woman every day.

Aside from the interpersonal conflict going on between me and asshole one and asshole two, I really don't feel like meditating. I did notice all the BS about inner peace and meditation on the website when I was booking. I planned to skip all of those parts and just go fish, or day drink, or do literally anything other than sit really still. The idea of being still and doing nothing for extended periods of time is like torture to me.

"I can't sit down. I was hit with a tree. And then by a man. I'm fucking sore. Sitting's not on my agenda."

"You got one stroke of the cane, and a few slaps, you absolute brat," Soren laughs. I'm glad he finds this funny, because I don't, and Jason doesn't either, but for very different reasons. Jason thinks I'm a spoiled brat. I think these controlling psychos lured me to a forest and are now toying with me.

"I don't want to meditate. I'm not going to meditate."

"This is a meditation retreat."

"Nuh uh."

"Yeah huh," Jason replies.

"It's not anymore," I say. "It's a fishing and leave-me-the-fuck-alone-until-the-boat-comes retreat now."

They look at one another. I know for absolute certain I am not worth the extreme waste of time it is going to be for them to make me do what's on the schedule. Sure, they're prepared to break out the kinky shit once or twice, but are they going to fight me every step of the way, every hour of the day? I don't think so. I'll wear these fuckers down before they know what happened to them. And then it occurs to me. Money might solve this.

"Tell you what," I say. "I'll tip fifty percent if the two of you leave me the fuck alone and bring me food from time to time."

That's got to be a good deal. They'd be crazy to turn it down. An extra five grand each to just chill in the forest? Yeah. It's a no-brainer.

They look at one another. That's right. There's more money where that first twenty grand came from. I wonder how much it'll cost to get Jason to kiss my ass.

"No."

"No? You don't want a little extra spending money? Buy yourselves some new camo pants and maybe somewhere comfortable to sleep?"

"Aslin. You're not listening," Soren says. "I know where you come from paying people off is obviously part of the lifestyle, but that won't work here. Here there's just one choice: doing as you're told."

Well, fuck that.

"I'm not sitting down. I'm not meditating. I'm not doing as I'm told. I'm not doing anything except what I feel like doing. You can get rid of me, you can call a boat for me, but you can't make me do anything."

"That's where we disagree," Jason says. "Now. Sit your ass down."

"No."

I can't afford to lose this battle of wills. If I lose this one, I'll lose all of them. That's why they're not backing down either.

"Aslin," Soren says. He's about to try to talk some sense into me, I can feel it. "On your application, you said you've been told you need to learn to relax."

That part is true. I saw a doctor before I came out here and he said if I didn't find a way to de-stress, I was going to have some real issues.

"I know I need to relax. That's why I brought the fishing rod and a case full of vodka."

"The fishing rod is fine. The vodka, not so much. We're here to teach skills that will last a lifetime. You'll be able to calm yourself in any situation, find your inner peace."

I laugh a little under my breath, because this guy has no fucking idea about my situation, or how remote the option of peace really is. I know what I said on the form. It was a fraction of a part of a portion of the truth. I keep my truth to myself.

"Sounds great," I say. I guess I'm giving in, but not because I'm going to do what they want, but because I really don't want to invite any more conversation about or interest in myself. At least meditation involves everybody shutting the hell up for a minute.

"Alright. Now. Let's sit."

I'm not giving in. I'm playing along. There's a difference. That's what I tell myself. I cross my legs and sink down toward the ground, putting my fingers in that smug little pose thing...

"FUCK!" I jump up as soon as I sit down. My ass is aching and as soon as I put my weight on it, it felt like I was getting spanked again all at once.

"I am not sitting down on that hard fucking..."

Jason looks pleased with himself. The only thing that takes the edge off his smugness is the way he's still damp from his dip in the river. We've both drawn metaphorical blood today.

"Alright," Soren relents. "You tried. Briefly. But I'll take it. Let's get you settled and have some food. Maybe that will improve the mood around here."

I'm still not seeing anything that makes me feel hopeful about the meal situation. This is a camp devoid of most things that are usually compatible with life. I don't see anywhere to sleep, anywhere to eat, or anywhere to... you know.

"What the fuck are we going to eat out here? I don't see a chef? Or a caterer."

"We have rations."

Jason goes to the center pillar which is built out with cabinetry. I guess having it in the center of the structure keeps things drier than they'd otherwise be. I take a glance inside and see that they really do have everything impeccably ordered. There are bedrolls stacked and folded. They don't look completely comfortable, but what here does? I wonder if they even have pillows, or if pillows are an impediment to inner peace. The blankets look like the scratchy old fashioned military kind. With every ocular revelation I contemplate another unspeakable horror.

Jason hands me one of the packs. Spaghetti Bolognese, apparently. "I'll show you how to add water so it heats up," he says.

I shake the thing in his face. "You've got to be fucking killing me. I paid twenty grand, and you're serving me two-dollar MREs?"

"You tell me where you can get MREs for two dollars," Jason grunts. "Ten bucks minimum."

"I'm not eating that stuff."

Jason's back to scowling at me. "Do you have to fight every-thing, all the time, every step of the way?"

"You're trying to feed me dog food!"

"Well, missy, if you're too spoiled to eat what's offered, you're free to provide your own food."

"Try the spaghetti," Soren says. "It's actually one of the better ones."

"One of the better ones. Not really selling me very hard here, you know," I sigh.

"Just try," he says in that eminently reasonable tone.

I have had a very long day. It was not easy getting here. I've been traveling for several days now. Conventional transport got me to Kathmandu, but since then I've been taking local options. I've been pulled by a donkey, I have accompanied chickens, I have hauled my luggage in and out of several boats, and I pepper sprayed two different men. I was looking forward to a nice room, a hot bath, and a good meal. Instead I've got absolutely nothing except a bloody mary on an empty stomach and a fucking foul mood. I can understand a bare bones service, but this doesn't even qualify as hospitality. It's the exact opposite of hospitality.

"No. Thank you." I hand the MRE back, and I go and sort my bags. I have a soft sweater that I can use to pad my ass a bit when I sit down. I have a lot of things. The fishing rod was a good idea, but I don't have that much else in the way of supplies. A few snacks, okay, a box of chocolate candy. But that's not going to last long out here. I knew I was going to have to fend for myself when I left New York, but I had no idea how much fending there would be.

3

She looks miserable. For the first time since she hit our camp like a hurricane, she's stopped being a ball of energy and instead she's going through her pink cases as if there's some chance the solution to being lost in the woods with Jason and me is in there.

I nudge Jason. "This isn't great."

"No," he says. "It's not. We should have picked the vlogger who wanted to record the whole thing for the Internet."

We chose Aslin for a reason, and I still believe in that reason. She needs our help. She's not been easy so far, but she's obviously smart, and therefore she can be talked to, reasoned with.

"I'm going to talk to her."

"Just let her sulk," he says. "She'll come around when she gets hungry enough. Let her settle in."

That's actually a good idea. I know he's not thrilled with our new guest, but he does have some good common sense when it comes to handling difficult people. I decide to leave her to it, and I start setting up the beds. First I unroll them, then I add the blankets and the pillows. The center pillar of the camp has a stone outcropping on one side where a fire can be lit without burning the entire thing down. And there are canvas drop downs on each of the open portions of the outer wall which can be closed in the case of bad weather. This might look primitive, but it's also a very cozy little place that most of our guests come to enjoy. I'm sure Aslin will be no different.

She just looks so lost, sitting there, sorting through her things. There's a faraway expression in her eyes, and a dismal pout to her lips. She's alone in the world. I can feel that loneliness emanating as night falls, something I feel in my gut. Aslin is pretty, in a girl-next-door sort of way. She has those big, deep, soulful eyes, and that oak-toned hair that falls into her eyes every time she lowers her head. I can tell she likes to look after herself. Her fingernails are very well manicured for an expert fisherwoman. She's a little bit of a mystery, and I like that. I notice that there's a thin line of pale skin on her left ring finger. She was wearing a ring there until recently. Interesting. A divorcee, then, or perhaps a broken engagement. That would explain the attitude and latent hostility.

"Can I help you with something?" She gives me a stare.

"Just thought you might like someone to talk to. I know it's an adjustment coming out here, especially if you've had a lot of changes and stress in your life recently."

"Okay, Psychic Dan," she says, rolling her eyes at me. There's a part of me that needs to whip the attitude out of her. But there's a bigger part that feels her pain. As hard as Jason and I come across, we do this because we want to help people. In a remote location. Away from society as a whole. "You can stop trying to make friends with me. I'm not interested. I didn't come to talk to anyone, especially a man. I wanted to be left alone. Can you do that for me? Can you leave me to myself?"

Aslin

Well, now I feel bad. He goes away when I ask, without giving me any of the attitude I gave him in return. He seems like a really nice guy. He's gorgeous too, and charming, and he has that earnestness about him that only good people have, not to mention he pays attention. So many men don't pay any kind of attention at all.

This is too much. I don't have enough energy to deal with an emotionally interested and possibly sexually available hot guy. Jason, on the other hand, he gives me jungle fuck boy vibes. He might be good for a vacation fling.

It's better for Soren to learn now that I'm not someone he should get involved with. I want to be a red flag factory where he is concerned. And really, the sooner I can get out of here, the better. It's not what I thought it was going to be, and with just the three of us out here all I can think about is how obvious my emotional baggage is going to be. I need to go somewhere else.

"Do you really not have a boat?" I call the question out to Jason. "I'd like to get out of here tonight."

"Not happening," he calls back. "Got your MRE if you want it and your bed when you're ready."

"We all just sleep out in the open like animals?"

"We sleep by the fire. Smoke keeps the bugs away and keeps us warm through the night. It's nice."

Soren has gone off into the jungle. I wonder if I hurt his feelings. I was pretty short with him. Then again, it doesn't matter. I'm getting out of here as soon as possible. Maybe I'm getting out of here before it's possible. All I have to do is get back to the village I came from. Now yes, I technically came upriver because it's the only way to get here, but there's no reason I can't walk along the riverbank.

"I'm heading out," I say. It's going to be annoying with two suitcases, but I'd rather be annoyed and get out of this dead end than stay here and let these two force me into their wholesome military mindfulness cult with a side of spanking.

"Aslin, come sit by the fire." Soren emerges from the forest with wood under his arm. Jason doesn't say anything. He just looks at me balefully.

"I'm leaving," I tell him. "Thanks for everything, and yeah, nothing."

"Come and sit. You signed yourself into our care when you signed up for this trip, and we're going to keep you here until we can get you safely back on an approved transport."

"You mean that rickety piece of shit boat? I'll be fine."

"Aslin," Soren says my name again. Every time he does, I feel a bolt of sensation rushing down my spine. "If you don't do as I'm telling you, I am going to punish you."

"Oh, fuck off you are. If you so much as put a finger on me, I'll make you eat it. I'm done with this bullshit."

"You paid a lot of money to not have that option. Now. Come here."

"No."

Soren unloads his wood and comes for me. I ditch my bags, because I can't move with them nearly as easily. All I have going for me is my agility.

"Get away from me!" I squeal the words as he comes closer. I can tell he's going to try to grab me. Mr Big Man wants to prove a point.

"Come here, and I won't have to do this," he says. "You're acting like a spoiled little girl, and I am about to treat you like one."

"Fuck off you are." I really thought that Jason would be the one to do something like this. He seems like the hunter type, the dominant kind, the one who demands obedience. Instead, it's Soren who is taking the lead here, making me submit to him, and to the stupid agreement I made.

"You're overtired," he says, his voice deep, but with a hint of sympathy. "You need to rest, not set off on a death march. These forests are full of wild animals, and the terrain and climate are both dangerous."

I'm not listening to him. I just want to get away. I am in flight mode. Have been for a longer time than anybody here knows. The closer he gets, the more intensely I feel the need to be away. From here. From anywhere. It doesn't matter where I end up, I just have to be at a distance.

I try to run into the forest, but he's too fast for me. Soren gives chase, and the forest itself is not exactly friendly. It's thicker than I expected, and it sort of repels me as I attempt to run through it.

"C'mere, you," Soren says as he grabs me and throws me over his shoulder, carrying me back to Camp Gazebo.

"Put me down! Put me fucking down!"

"You'll go down over my knee," he says seriously. "You're getting a spanking and then I'm putting you to bed. There aren't many rules here, but not running off into the forest when night is falling is one of them."

He sits down on the edge of the gazebo and pulls me into that humiliating position. It's so fucking intimate. I can feel every bit of him, every hard line of his stomach and thighs, every soft piece of me pressing against all of it.

"No!" I shout

"Yes," he says. He's just holding me, keeping me where he wants me. I have this horrible feeling in the pit of my stomach, like I know what is about to happen is going to really hurt, and that I maybe truly deserve it too, and that he's going to do it.

Jason did this before, but it happened quickly. It was over almost before I knew it had started, and I was in fight mode when it happened. It felt different than this.

"I don't know your story," Soren says. "But I hope I'll learn it as we get to know each other. For now, you need to know that all I care about is keeping you safe, even from decisions you think you want to make. As long as you're here in my care, that's what my job is."

I take a deep breath. His words are freaking me out way more than the actions. Pain doesn't scare me. Someone getting overly involved in my personal drama does. Soren has no idea about me. The responsibility he thinks he wants would crush him in an instant if he knew what it was.

"Soren," I say, as calm as I can. "This is not a good idea."

He adjusts me over his lap, lifting my ass a little higher, and putting my head a little lower. His palm smooths over my pants. It doesn't dip down into the crevice between my cheeks. He's a gentleman. Fuck. I don't know what to do with a gentleman. Especially not one who seems intent on getting to know me and taking me to task. He might be the first person I ever met who didn't let me get away with everything. Between him and Jason, I'm suddenly lost.

"Please," I say, a little softer. "I'm sorry."

"I don't think you are. I know you're not. You're just realizing that out here being in trouble actually means something."

"Please, Soren. Don't. Please."

I'm begging. I'm actually begging. I don't know how much a spanking is going to hurt, but I know for sure I can't deal with all the emotional intensity of it. There's something about this guy that gets under my skin. I've known him one day, and I'm absolutely fucking lost.

"You really don't want to be given a spanking, do you? Have you been punished before? I mean, before you got here?"

"Not like this."

"Alright, so. Here's how this happens..."

"No! No! No..." I start squirming and wriggling for all I am worth. I have to get off his lap.

"Okay, easy, easy." He pulls me back into place with one hand at the base of my spine, gripping the jumpsuit. This garment makes me way too easy to control. I need to invest in something more tearaway. "Settle down, baby."

"I'm not a baby! I'm not your baby! Lemme go. Now!" My voice is reaching a pitch so high even I can't hear it anymore.

"Let her go."

I never expected Jason to come to my aid, but he picks me up bodily off Soren's lap, puts me down on the ground while keeping hold of my arm, and proceeds to spank me hard with six hard smacks to each of my cheeks.

"There," he says, as I dance and writhe in his grasp. "You've had a spanking. Go get in bed. Now."

I can't believe it, but I do as I'm told. I'm all too pleased to scurry away from both men. Soren is fucking intense. Too intense. Jason is confrontational and mean, but he's simple. He doesn't get under my skin. He doesn't get in my head. He just smacks my ass and makes demands I then fail to fulfill. I know where I am with him. I have no idea where I will end up with Soren.

. . .

J*ason*

"What was that?"

Soren asks me the question once we've got her in bed and probably asleep. She's quiet at least, and we know where she is. With this girl, that feels like a triumph.

Soren's a smart guy, but he has no idea what to do with this brat. He's overwhelming her by trying to be sensitive with her.

"She's sensitive," I explain. "That's why you've got to be rough with her."

"What the hell do you mean?"

"I mean if you're all intense and slow and insist on talking about feelings, she's going to freak out."

"So your suggestion is not to bother with her feelings or try to get through to her in a more meaningful way. It's just smack her ass and send her to bed?"

"Exactly."

"It's that simple?"

"Yep," I tell him. "It's that simple."

4

Aslin

I wake up in the middle of the night with no idea where I am. I wake Jason and Soren up as well, on account of the fact I'm screaming. This happens from time to time. It's not something that usually bothers anybody, but I'm not usually sleeping in an open-walled gazebo with two military men.

Upon hearing my incoherent shrieks, they startle awake. Jason is on his feet and reaching for a weapon. Soren doesn't go for a gun; he comes for me instead.

"What's wrong?" Soren wraps his arms around me.

"I want to go home." I don't sound powerful anymore. I sound small, and scared. It's a lie. I don't want to go home. I want to get as far away from home as humanly possible. I would have thought this was it, but the demons have followed me into the night. There's really no escaping what I left behind. Even when I consciously forget it, it comes back to get me when I have no control over my mind at all.

"I know," Soren soothes me, patting my ass. "It's okay to feel homesick. It's normal, even. This is a very different world for you, in a lot of ways."

He's way too nice. He has no idea what is going on with me, or what darkness follows. He's so prepared to view me as a helpless little girl with a nightmare. Fine. I'm not explaining myself to him. I can't even imagine how that would go. He'd lose his fucking mind.

I'm starting to feel a little better. The human contact is nice. Very soothing. Especially the way his big hand keeps sliding back and forth over my rear, soothing away the same spanking he gave me a couple hours ago. Outside the gazebo the stars are calm, and the breeze is cool. Everything is okay. I don't know how, or why. But everything is okay.

"Time to sleep now. You don't need to go anywhere tonight. Tonight, all you need to do is relax," Soren says. He pulls his roll over to mine and embraces me as if we've known one another for months, or maybe even years. The easy intimacy is a little confusing. Is this part of the service they offer? Are they jungle gigolos? I'm guessing not. If they were, they'd probably be more amenable to being paid off.

I'm not in the mood to question this right now. I'm getting what I need, somehow. It almost feels magical. I let Soren pull me close. I let him snug me against his shirtless body. I take what he's offering, and I hope it is not a huge mistake.

I feel safe for the first time in a long time.

And I sleep.

~

"Up. Get. Up."

I open my eyes to a rough demand in the dark. Okay, not the dark. There are hints of day on the distant horizon. At first, I don't know what's going on. I think it's something terrible. My fingers curl into a fist, and that fist shoots straight out from under the covers and catches my assailant dead center of his handsome face. There's a crunching sound, followed by a rough curse.

"Fucking hell!" Jason rocks back on his knees, both hands on his nose.

It's not broken, but it has made his eyes water. Serves him right for waking me up like that. I don't know where Soren is, but I know Jason's going to be mad as hell. I have not made a good first, second, or third impression here.

"What the fuck are you doing?" I ask the question aggressively. Some people might apologize for punching a guy in the face, but I'm not going to.

"It is time to meditate," he says.

"I said I'd pay you if you'd shut up about that bullshit. What is this, a shakedown?"

"I'm not taking a bribe," Jason declares. "I'm going to do my job instead."

"Why!?"

"Because I like my job, and I don't like being dismissed by a spoiled brat who thinks she can buy her way out of every inconvenience."

"So you admit this is an inconvenience."

He picks me up under the arms and hefts me physically out of bed. Cold air rushes in, waking me up instantly all the way.

"Ugh!"

He carries me from the gazebo and eventually deposits me on a cushion on the dock. Soren is already sitting cross-legged on the one next to it. I don't have the energy to fight first thing in the morning. I need coffee to get me into true combat mode.

The world is still. The water in the river flows by with soft sounds. Occasionally, an insect chirps or a bird flutters. The world around us is alive with its own little intentions. I just want to go back to sleep.

My eyelids drift down time and time again. The next thing I'm aware of is Soren nudging me up to my feet.

"Alright," he says. "Good work."

"Sleeping on the dock isn't good work," Jason grumbles, but I think he's secretly pleased. Nobody is trying to whip me with the scenery, so that's a good sign. Maybe we just all got off on the wrong foot yesterday. That happens to me kind of a lot. I'm not really what you might call someone who makes good first impressions.

"Breakfast time," Soren declares.

I am starving, but I'm still not prepared to eat one of their MREs. Fortunately that's not on the menu. Instead they've managed to rustle up some eggs and rice. It's simple, but it's good.

"So. What are we doing today? Constructing wind chimes? Observing our inner selves?" I sass the question in the direction of either of the men.

"We're going on a hike up the mountain," Jason says.

I let out a deep sigh. "You are full of ideas of things I do not want to do. At all."

"Why did you sign up for this retreat if you just wanted to do your own thing? You could have rented a cabin on a lake and not had to deal with any of this."

Soren's question is insightful, and that is why I do not like it.

"I assumed most of it would be optional. These things are usually bullshit. Some nonsense on some website. Promises of relaxation and maybe enlightenment. It's all the same kind of lie. I had no reason whatsoever to believe you'd be out here taking things seriously."

"Surprise," Jason deadpans.

"My offer is still good. Five grand each and I get to do whatever I want, and so do you. It's the best deal you're going to get. You guys don't want to be out here babysitting me. I'm a handful at the best of times, and nothing about this is the best of times."

I look between the two of them. Five grand will go a long way out here, and it's for three weeks of work, which is very good deal.

"Come on, boys," I say. "Can't tell me you wouldn't like to sleep in and have a break. Could take a break from this wilderness and go to Kathmandu. Hit some bars. Find some girls. Hmm?" I waggle my brows in what I hope is a suggestive way.

"I'm not taking your bribe," Jason growls.

"Fine. I'll double it. Ten grand each, and I don't have to go on a hike."

"You have to stop trying to buy your way out of everything."

"I bought my way into this mess. Why can't I buy my way out of it?"

"There is a certain logic to that," Soren admits.

Jason disagrees. "No. My services are for sale specifically within the parameters of the contract. I am not available for paid vacations. If I wanted to let spoiled brats run amok, I'd go work in a daycare. We chose to run this retreat the way we run it with the rules we established for it. We were very clear on what you were signing up for. Your regret is not my problem, and you cannot bribe your way out of it."

"So Jason's a man of principle for no apparent reason; what about you, Soren? You don't have anything you could spend ten grand on?" I reply.

"It's not going to work, Aslin," Soren says.

"Yes. Alright. I see. Okay. Great. Let's hike a mountain, then."

~

They're serious about this, and I guess that means I have to be too. I did pack some sensible boots, thinking I might need to make a getaway over rough terrain at some point. That means I'm ready to go for a hike with them when they demand I go on a hike with them. They don't know me well enough to know that my compliance is a cover for a greater plan to do whatever I want after all.

We walk for several minutes, which I don't love but can handle. Then, about fifteen minutes down the trail, there's a turn off in the goat path. It goes off our route and starts winding up the hillock a little.

"What's up there?"

"Local village," Jason says. "The locals call it Ramro."

A local village. Perfect. That means civilization of one kind or another. See, I knew this wouldn't really be that far out. I bet they made me take the boat upriver for so long to try to create an air of remoteness, but in reality there's probably an interstate over the next ridge. This is all a big scam. Everything is always a big scam.

Including the shit I'm about to pull.

I offered to pay my way out of the situation, but I guess no-more-Miss-Nice-Guy is the way we're going to go instead. I'm not going to fight with them. Obviously I'll lose any direct confrontation. But they have to know I'm in no shape to climb a mountain. I mentally dub this plan: Operation Pathetic.

As the incline grows steeper, I take a dive. I make it look good, too. A tree root becomes the scapegoat of my imagined accident. I tumble awkwardly over with a high-pitched yowl and grab immediately at my foot.

"My ankle!" I gasp. "My ankle hurts so much."

They don't know this, but one of my ankles is perpetually swollen from an injury when I was much younger. It's not so much swelling as it is scar tissue that becomes a little inflamed and, well, anyway, I have a puffy ankle and I know how to work it.

They both stop. Jason looks at me with an expression I find hard to read. Soren goes to his knees beside me, blue eyes full of concern. I lay it on thick, whimpering, but not crying. You don't want to pretend to cry if you can't produce tears. That's a rookie mistake.

"It hurts," I whine.

"Shh. It's okay," Soren comforts me. "Let's get that boot off."

"Shouldn't take that off until we get back. Her leg'll swell up and we won't be able to get the boot back on," Jason says. He's trying to pretend he's not concerned, but he's concerned.

"It doesn't look so bad. I don't see any bruising."

There's never going to be any bruising. But he doesn't know that. This is working. I can't believe it's actually working.

"We're heading back to camp," he says. "Want a piggyback?"

I wrap my arms around his neck and rest my head on his shoulder. I don't really have any choice. It's hard to keep my head up while he carries me back toward the camp. I'm a little sad that I pulled this shit so soon. They're a lot quicker going back to camp than they were going out from it, so I get approximately five minutes clinging to Soren's muscular back, my legs supported by his strong arms. Five minutes of feeling as safe as I ever have.

"Alright," he says, setting me down back at Camp Gazebo. "We're going to make you comfortable.

I didn't count on this. This feeling. Guilt. Why the fuck do I feel guilty?

It's because he's being so nice, that's why. I knew this would be a good way to get out of being compelled on an unwanted death march up the hill, but I didn't think it would force me to confront my own lack of what I guess you'd call morality. It's not nice to manipulate nice people. Soren might be a nice guy. Hell, Jason might be a nice guy too.

Oh no. Does that mean that I'm the bad guy?

I might be the bad guy.

I might always have been the bad guy.

Soren

I know she's faking. When someone is in real pain, their face goes pale and their eyes go wide and there's a tension in their body that you can't miss. Aslin was complaining, but she wasn't truly in pain. That might change later.

"You're so nice," she says, looking at me almost bewildered. "Why are you being so nice?"

She's adorable. A huge brat, but adorable.

"Because you deserve it," I say. It's true, even if she doesn't understand why. Even if she thinks she's not worth the kindness, or the discipline, or the time. Even if she wants to be left alone because she's certain nobody could understand her, even if they wanted to.

"You have no idea what I deserve," she says, looking at me under her lashes.

"Soren!" Jason yells my name. I go over to him, as he clearly doesn't want to discuss this in front of her.

"Yeah?"

"She's fucking with us," Jason says. "There's nothing wrong with that ankle."

"Yes. She is."

"You're not going to call her out on it?"

"No," I say. "We spent most of the first day spanking her ass, and what did that achieve? She defied us, tried to bribe us, now she's trying to cheat us. It's like the stages of grief, except it's her coming to terms with not getting her own way."

"Except she is getting her own way," Jason points out. "She's getting out of the hike, and she thinks we're stupid. I don't like playing games."

"She's pretending to not be able to move very far or very fast. She's basically put herself into a mandatory meditation. At least, that's how I intend to play it."

Jason smirks. "Good idea."

~

We have lunch, and she eats without complaint. I'm guessing she feels guilty for trying to pull one over on us. Or maybe she just got hungry enough to stop whining. It's like Jason says, keep things simple.

"Alright, now we'll spend the rest of the afternoon meditating," I announce. "That's something we can do without moving, so your ankle won't be a problem."

"An entire afternoon meditating?" Her eyes go wide. "I can't survive that."

"Of course you can," Jason says. He's tagging in, and after yesterday's meltdown when I tried to spank her deserving little ass, maybe that's a good thing. The two of us make a great team, not quite good cop/bad cop, but something of the kind.

Aslin

"I don't want to sit around not thinking," I say. "I think I should lie back, keep my ankle elevated, and just take it easy."

"I think you should keep your ankle elevated and do as I tell you," he says. I'm not going to get out of this if I keep my pretense up. They're going to assume that I can't do anything except meditate, and that's my worst fucking nightmare. I think I'd rather hike than sit still. I'd do almost anything rather than sit still.

"Okay, fine. I lied. My ankle doesn't hurt."

"I know your ankle doesn't hurt. Something else is going to hurt very soon, though." Jason is glowering down at me like a vengeful forest spirit.

"More of your caning and punishment?"

"Probably. But I think there's something else to take from you. Something you promised not to bring when you filled out your application. I know you planned to ignore that from the outset, but it matters to me."

"What is it, then?"

Jason walks over to my things and picks up the little case I keep for emergencies. The case with the flasks and the shaker. The case I keep to take the edge off when the world gets too sharp. He carries it down to the dock, and I know what he's going to do with it. He's going to sink my drink.

"No! Not that!" I chase after him, limping for a few steps out of habit of pretending to be injured, before running properly. It doesn't matter. He's already by the water, unzipping my case, taking my flask out and uncapping it.

"You're not drinking again as long as you're here. You don't need it, and you definitely don't deserve it. Remember this next time you decide to pull something."

"You can use your belt," I plead. "You can use whatever you like. I won't even try to stop you. Just don't throw my booze away. You have no idea how much that matters."

"I can, and will, use whatever I want on you. I'm also tossing the booze. You need to learn your lesson. This might finally help you do that."

He throws it away. He fucking throws it away. Sploosh! It goes into the river with a surprisingly resonant sound. It hits me right in the gut.

"NO!"

I throw myself after the flask. I can get it before it sinks to the bottom, I know I can. I'm not letting Jason come between me and my alcohol friends.

Jason

I guess we're not done yet. I guess we're just getting started.

Aslin surfaces with the flask in her hand. I watch, annoyed, as she pulls the stopper out with her teeth, spits it into the river, and proceeds to drink as much as possible. She's paddling with one arm, kicking to stay afloat, and pouring alcohol down her throat as fast as she can.

She's making a point. Not the point she thinks she's making, either. All I'm taking from this is that Aslin will kill herself just to defy me. She's more than a brat. I don't know if there actually is a word for what she is.

Not stupid, at least. The current is carrying her away, but because she's not fighting it, and sheer luck, it takes her to a bank about half a mile away. Only problem? It's the other bank. And that means she just stranded herself unless she wants to take another swim.

This doesn't bother Aslin, because she doesn't realize how badly she's fucked herself over yet. Right now, she thinks she has won. She stands on the bank, sopping wet, gripping her flask and shouting at me. When she realizes I might not be able to hear every word, she supplements her shrill triumphant cries with unmistakable middle-fingered gestures.

And that's when Soren decides to show up again. I'm standing with my arms folded over my chest, watching this chaos unfold. He comes up, open mouthed.

"What the..." Soren stares. "I was gone for five minutes!"

"A lot can happen in five minutes."

"What is she, Jackie Sparrow over there with the rum?"

She's waving to him now. Then she turns around, bends over forwards, and sort of waves her ass at us. The material of her pants is clinging to her cheeks in a lewd sort of way, but I don't know if she's just not a very good dancer, or if the drink has stunted her coordination, but she starts shaking her ass.

"What is she doing?" I turn to Soren. He seems to understand her spoiled rich girl motivations better than I do.

"I think that's twerking."

"That's terrible twerking."

We laugh. She's making an absolute fool of herself, and she has no idea. She thinks she's won something, but night is falling, she has no real provisions, and she's wet to the skin. That's a good way to die in any remote location. She might be alright if she got out of the wet clothes, made a fire, and warmed up, but I'm going to go way out on a limb and say she couldn't make a fire with a box of matches.

Soren starts making a plan. "We've got to get her back, sober her up, and..."

"And what? Tie her up? She doesn't want to listen. We've smacked her ass how many times, and all she's done is act out more."

"When the enemy escalates, you escalate."

"She's not the enemy. I think we need a little de-escalation."

"She's going to read that as weakness," I tell him. We've tried every civilized means of getting through to her, and a whole lot of old school discipline. It's not working. The more she gets, the more she wants. I'd bet my paycheck, plus the bonus bribe, that this girl likes pain more than most."

Soren sighs. "I hate to say it, but I think you're right. What do you want to do?"

"Half-measures aren't working. Follow my lead. And trust me."

5

slin

They've got a boat. It was covered by some sacks at the side of the river, I guess to hide it from the person who insisted on leaving the second she got here. What *assholes.*

The pair of them are paddling across the river, both shirtless. They ripple and gleam in the sunlight reflected off the water's surface. They're so hot. So very, very sexy. It probably says something about my psyche that my level of attraction to them increases with how much I've annoyed them.

Right now, they both look either very unimpressed or outright pissed off. They keep paddling all the way up to the bank, and instead of stopping the boat next to the bank, they run it up on it, making the boat skid in a particularly cool way.

"Whoa!" I exclaim, holding the remnants of my flask aloft. There're just a few dregs left, but I feel particularly attached to them. And particularly in a good mood. I'm not drunk, per se, but I am happy. And not overly concerned with consequences.

Jason leaps out of the boat and grabs me by the upper arm. His grip is like a vise. There's no escaping it, even if I wanted to. I don't think I want to. He drags me closer to him and glares down at me with furious eyes. I laugh, mostly because I'm drunk, but also somewhat because I'm nervous. I have that feeling in the very pit of my stomach, like I have truly fucked up now. There has to be a limit past which they'll give up on me and just send me home. That would be kind of a point of pride, but it would sting too.

"You're such a little shit," he curses.

"Yeah," I agree, though probably with more cheer and pride than he'd like. Then I remember I actually have something to yell at them about.

"You said I had to wait for a boat to leave!"

"You can't row your way back down river. You need a motorboat. And a local guide. If you want to really die out here, take the boat, get lost on the river. Now. Shut up."

"Rude."

He drags me back to the boat by my arm, but not before wresting the empty flask from me. He hands that off to Soren, who is standing there looking disappointed in me. That hurts a bit. Why would he be disappointed? It's not as though I've set any standards for sane behavior so far.

"Sit down, don't move. We don't want to capsize. This river is full of dangerous beasts."

"Only beasts I see are in the boat with me."

I'm teasing. They're mad. I'm not. I'm finally having a good time, maybe because I'm drunk. I know that sooner or later the buzz will wear off, and at that time I'll feel bad about it all. For now, though, I am queen of the jungle.

The journey back across the river is swift. At the other side, they get me out and pull the boat up to the dock. I wonder what will happen next, what painful humiliation is planned for me now.

I look between Jason and Soren. Jason is glowering at me. Soren is barely making eye contact. He seems preoccupied.

"I'm going to go collect wood and supplies," Soren says. "You got her?"

"I've got her," Jason confirms.

"Don't leave me alone with him!" I cry out. God knows what Jason is capable of without Soren to make him behave himself. Soren is like our mutual link to sanity. Left to our own devices, we're two sets of equal and opposite bad decisions.

"No point calling for him," Jason says. "You've pushed past the point of no return now. You just had to test me, didn't you?"

"I wasn't testing you. I was getting my alcohol. You had no right..."

He's tying me up. I guess I must have drunk a lot, because I'm only just noticing that now he has my wrists bound with hemp rope. And that's not where he stops. He dumps me on the ground using his fancy military martial arts and proceeds to do the same to my ankles. I could be fighting him more than I am, but I'm buzzed and bemused. Plus, the way his big hands feel sliding over my limbs as he works the rope around them is not exactly unpleasant. Jason's a beast. An absolute unit.

He picks me up, trussed like a smug, happy chicken, and puts me over one of the rolled-up bedrolls so my hips are raised. We all knew this was coming. There's no pleasure without pain. There's no beating Jason without also losing to him.

I turn my face so I'm not looking directly at the floor, and I see him standing over me. He's taken his belt off and is looping the dark, thick, oiled leather around his hand, leaving a long tail, all the better to beat me with.

He leaves me clothed in my tank top and pants, but that hardly matters. Wet clothing transmits the effects of his belt with a wild intensity that makes me scream. Jason doesn't spank me. He thrashes me. Hard. The motion of his arm rising and falling, not to mention the twist of his hips makes for a frightening shadow cast over me. I feel chills and goosebumps along with heat and fury.

"What the fuck bondage bullshit is this?" I scream out between strokes. I need him to stop, or at least to slow down. Jason is no fucking joke. He's capable of doing more damage than he's doing, I'm sure, but I don't know how much of his punishment I can take — though I know I deserve it all.

"It's to keep you from being a danger to yourself," Jason says. "You make the worst decisions of any person I have ever known."

"How is that possible when you've been to war?" I sniff the question. I'm caught between tears and something else.

"Do you want me to compare you to a war zone, Aslin? Is that how destructive and damaging you want to be? Would make a lot of sense."

"No. I mean... no."

His hand drifts over my ass. It's still aching and sore, because that's what a belt applied to the same region with the strength of a pissed off ex-military man will do to you. I know I deserved everything I got. Maybe I even wanted what I got. Maybe I was wondering how far they'd go. I might have some of my answer.

Jason's fingers curl around the cleft of my ass, the middle finger brushing against a very tight, very private region. I don't know if he meant to do that. Then he does it again, and I'm sure he did mean to do it. He is toying with my ass, with the one place I swore I'd never let any man go.

"You're a bad girl, Aslin, and I don't think we can punish you into being a good girl." His lips are very close to my ear. "I don't think you respond to force. I think you resist punishment because secretly, or not so secretly, you crave it."

His fingers press more firmly between my ass cheeks. I feel the tip of his middle finger rubbing the fabric of my underwear against the tight hole. I should have known he was an ass man. I'm surprised he wants to touch me. I thought by now he'd hate me. From the moment we met, I've been pushing his buttons. More than pushing. I've been shoving them. Hard. Now it's time for him to push back. The button he's choosing is a very different one. It's sensitive. Soft. Hidden.

I let out a moan. I can't help myself. Rationally, I know I should resist, tell him to stop, demand that he leave me alone. But I don't want him to leave me alone. I haven't been testing and taunting him all this time to be shy now.

*J*ason

Before I can get her as naked as we both need her to be, Soren returns with an armful of wood for the fire and a glare for me. I knew he'd object. He's got a thing for her. You'd have to be blind not to see it.

"What the fuck do you think you're doing? We don't grope the guests."

"Yeah, and we don't hold them after they tell us they want to go home, either. We both know we've made things so hard people bailed in the first week. And we kept her. Even when she screamed at us and told us to bring the boat back. We fucking kept her."

Soren scowls at me. That has gone unsaid for so long. We've never acknowledged that out loud. We went along with it together, because we both thought she was cute as hell and we both wanted to keep her in our orbit, even if she was trouble.

"We might have kept her," he agrees. "But I never said you could take her."

"So this is about sharing.'"

"This is about..."

He doesn't want to say it. Soren likes to be the good guy. He doesn't want to admit he wants to fuck our tied up little girl just as bad as I want to. That doesn't gel with his image of himself. So he's going to make me the bad guy. Unless I can make him the worse guy.

"We can share her. Let's be real. She's more than one man can handle."

"Does she want to be shared?"

"She's lying on the ground with that hemp wrapped around her, and she hasn't even tried to escape. The same girl who leaped into the river to grab her booze is lying there with her pants down, waiting for us to do something to her."

"She's tied up, Jason."

"She'd have wriggled away or mouthed off or something by now if she didn't want this. I rubbed her ass, and she wriggled back against me. She wants this."

I want my cock buried inside her. Not her pussy. Her ass. I want that tight, dark, bad little hole to spread for me. I'd bet good money she's never let any guy fuck her ass before. She's too much of a ball breaker for that.

"I'm going to go fuck her," I tell him. "You're welcome to join."

Soren's eyes narrow. "Be my guest," he grits out between clenched teeth.

I want to finish what I started with Aslin. I want to give her what we both need. I don't care if he approves or not. I know what I need to do.

I walk back to her and pull her wet pants and panties down in one motion. They peel off her pink ass, revealing everything I've wanted since the moment I met her. Tight holes.

Sweet cheeks. Vulnerability. Rebellion begging to be conquered.

"What are you doing?" Her question is breathy and soft and eager.

"Your ass," I tell her, spreading the lube over that winking little star, feeling it give for me and then resist again. She doesn't really know what she wants. All she knows is that she needs to be filled because she's a bad little girl.

There's a tightness between her cheeks. The lube helps my finger slide into the dark little hole there. A lot of men would go for her cunt, thinking that claiming her pussy would make her theirs, get her under control. But it's her ass that really matters, that really means something. I want this clenching hole, the one that grips my finger like it will miss it when it is gone.

She's squirming while tied up, breathing in short little gasps and grinding her pussy against the bedroll. She'd do anything for me to treat her pussy to my cock, but I have my target on lock. It's this hole or nothing. It's her ass, but my hole to take.

Soon enough, she starts to relax. Her spanked cheeks, her puffy pussy, her submissive position all play a role. I am making the good thing easy, and the wrong thing hard. The good thing is for her to give me her gorgeous little ass. The wrong thing is to try to stop me from punishing her for her disobedience.

My finger is not enough. Not for me, and not for her. My cock is fucking hard, and my balls are swollen. I need to be inside her, and she needs to be punished. I push the head of my cock to that sacrificial hole and claim what is mine, listening to her muffled grunts with real pleasure.

It's a tight fit, but the lube is good, and her ass stretches for me like it was made to stretch. Slowly, and with difficulty. Her whimpers make me even fucking harder. She's such a bad girl, and I am treating her like one.

I reach down and push her face against the floor. I want to make this demeaning. I want her to feel her place. I want to be rough, and yes, a little cruel. I want to be the monster my gut has been telling me she needs from the beginning.

I hear her grunt as I drive deeper, then she moans. She can't help it. She's drooling against the floor, her ass held high though I'm not gripping her hot, belted cheeks anymore. She's keeping herself open for me, her fine fingers clasped to her ass, her hole nicely lubricated for my cock so that with every stroke it gets a little easier for us both.

Taking pity on her and rewarding her for her obedience, I reach around and grip her pussy, holding her beneath me, letting that wet cunt drench my fingers. She's soaked.

"I'm going to come in your ass," I tell her, rubbing her pussy. "I'm going to fill your little asshole up, and you're going to come for me like the dirty little girl you are."

Her hips are bucking. She's locked between my cock and my fingers. I spank and I rub, I find her clit and I pay special, rough attention to it. I rub harder, faster, I spank that naughty bud, and more than anything, I fuck her ass. I fuck her deep and hard. I fuck her until she screams and drools against her bedroll, until the birds take fright and fly away, until her legs shiver and shudder, and until we both find desperate, dark release.

I pull out, not because I want to be free of her, but because I need to see her as she is now. I need to see her exposed, flushed cheeks, still held by her delicate fingers, and the smears of cum over her ass, a few drops on her pussy lips. She looks ravaged, and broken, and claimed. She looks perfect.

I spank her ass one last time and walk away.

A *slin*

He's left me tied up and filled with his cum. He's left me here, vulnerable to anybody who might see me. There is some part of me that hopes Soren will come next. My pussy has been deprived of cock. My ass has been punished inside and out. I am a very bad girl who got some of what she had coming.

Soren doesn't come. I can't see him, but I can hear the sounds of work going on around the camp. I have been left here on display, probably as part of my punishment. It's hot. It's hot to lie here, bound and drenched in cum. I'm still floating on clouds of arousal and endorphins, breathing in the scent of my own need. Jason made me confront my basest desires, and then he took me one step down.

"Alright," he says, returning after half an hour or so, freshly dressed and fully showered. He kneels down beside me and loosens my bindings enough for me to be able to get up. "Go get cleaned up, brat, and say sorry to Soren too."

"Am I apologizing for the drinking and swimming, or for what we did?"

"Apologize for whatever you most feel guilty for," he advises, slapping my ass. It hurts more now that the feel-good drugs of natural desire and the shots I managed to down have both worn off.

I get up and walk to the shower naked. I can't see Soren. Is he giving me privacy? That would be the gentlemanly thing to do, and I think he likes to be a gentleman.

The shower is lukewarm, the same temperature as the air around me. I wash myself with the pink loofah and body wash I brought with me, and I muse over all that has happened between Jason, Soren, and me.

I needed to get laid. And I think I needed the rest of it too, maybe even the bindings. I needed to feel like someone was actually in fucking charge for once. Jason has left me in no uncertain place about that, and though I won't thank him outright, I am grateful.

But I feel something else too... guilt. I don't know why. I have nothing to feel guilty about. But every time I see Soren's face, I feel... I don't know. There's something in me that's starting to have a very hard time with being who I am around these men.

The day is starting to wane by the time I get out of the shower and dress myself again. It's been a big one. So many lies. So much rebellion. So much fucking hot sex. My eyelids are heavy already, but I need to talk to Soren. He's back now and tending the fire in the gazebo.

S oren

Aslin is sheepish with me after all is said and done. I know she's not sorry for leaping into the river, for defying us and disobeying us. She's forgotten about all of that entirely. Jason erased all of it with his cock in a very sensitive part of her anatomy. All she can think about is the shame of that sex. I know that because she creeps up to me blushing at the very thought of what she and he did.

"So. Uhm. Me and Jason..."

"I know," I say. There's no point pretending this is some kind of secret.

"So, you're, what, angry at me for sleeping with Jason?"

She's defensive. Guilty. She should be, but not about Jason.

"I'm not angry."

"Good. Because I can fuck who I like."

"Seems more like anybody who likes to can fuck you."

Okay, that was a little harsh. Maybe there is a bit of sting there from hearing her give herself to Jason and from wanting to tag in. My conscience wouldn't let me. It would be so easy for us to use her, for her to forget what her will is and to just surrender to lust. I still think we're here for something a little higher and more important than sex.

She scowls at me. "Don't try to shame me. It won't work. I don't have a sense of shame."

"That's true," I agree — though I am not sure it is true. I think she is embarrassed by what she did with Jason. I think she's come to me for some kind of approval, or forgiveness, a little girl hoping Daddy isn't too mad at her.

I was jealous, at first. But the way she's looking at me now tells me she cares just as much about me and my opinions as she does Jason. She wants me too. She thinks if I have sex with her as well, she'll finally be in control. That's what it was really about, using her body to addle the minds of the men who seemed to be in charge. I think it worked. Jason has had a particularly goofy grin on his face since they were together.

"I'm not sorry," she adds defiantly.

"Good for you." I am smiling inwardly. I was so worried she had been taken advantage, or corrupted, or somehow changed by Jason's treatment. She's still the very same girl, my manipulative and sorry little Aslin who really wants nothing more than to be told she's actually a good girl after all.

"Why are you smiling?" She's scowling now. She's not getting the response she wants. The power isn't flowing the way she thought it would. She wanted me jealous. Instead, I'm controlled and self-contained. If I do ever choose to be with her, it will be on my terms, not hers. "You think I'm disgusting, don't you. You think you're better than me, because I have anal sex."

I sit, patiently, listening to her unload her fears on me, all the judgements she's worried I'll make about her coming out of her mouth rather than mine. She has no idea what I like sexually. None whatsoever. She's decided who she thinks I am, and she's very, very upset that that guy is judging her now.

"Ugh!" She throws up her hands and storms away, off to harangue Jason, no doubt. I'm sure that's going to go terribly for her.

A*slin*

Jason is sitting by the cooking fire with a bowl of rice with charred fish over the top. I bet it is bland as hell, but he's eating it like it's the best thing in the world.

"What's up?" He asks the question between swallows.

"You told him about the sex," I frown. I'm very upset but trying not to show it. I am not good at not showing it.

"Soren?"

"Yes. Now he thinks I'm disgusting."

"Uh. No. He doesn't." Jason keeps eating, his eyes more on his food than on me, though occasionally he'll cast a glance my way, just long enough to make eye contact.

"Yes. He does."

"He said that?"

"Well, no. But..."

"He doesn't think that." Jason speaks like he knows what Soren's thinking.

"How can you know?"

He sighs and moves his bowl slightly further away from his face. This feels like a dangerous thing.

"My god, woman, quit it already. Soren doesn't think any less of you for sex, anal or otherwise, because he's the kinkiest guy I know."

"No, he's not," I hear myself gasp. "He's so... so..."

Jason is looking at me with amusement, waiting for me to finish that sentence.

"So quiet!" I eventually say, though that makes no sense at all.

"It's the quiet ones you have to watch," he says, going back to his meal.

I don't believe him. "I don't believe you."

He grunts and shoos me away with his fork. I take the hint. My ass is more than sore enough, inside and out.

I retreat to a dark corner of the gazebo we live in, away from Jason and Soren, away from the flickering light of the fire and toward the shadows of my own thoughts.

I've lost track of time. How much longer before the boat comes? Will I be able to leave? Will I even want to leave? I'm more sober than I've been in months, if not years. The cool night air is making me feel clear-headed. I don't like what I'm getting clear on. I'm embarrassed that I let Jason take me that way, and even more embarrassed that Soren knows. I feel like I've lost some ground to them. Like they've gotten a little under my skin.

Sleep comes to me without warning, creeping up on me in a blanket of semi-tropical warmth.

. . .

Soren

"Sore, look at this."

Jason calls me to the far corner of the hut, where Aslin has curled up on a small pile of potato sacks like some kind of orphan waif in a Dickens novel. I guess she didn't want to go to bed on the rolls, which were much closer to us. It almost looks like there are tears dried on her cheeks. Did she cry herself to sleep from shame? Or something else?

"She is cute when she's asleep."

"Yeah," I agree.

"You still mad I got there first?"

"I'll be mad if you keep referring to her as a destination, and not a person."

"She wants you too, you know. She was so mad when she thought you'd lost interest in her."

"I don't know if we should be doing this. She's not a casual sort of girl. This could turn dark if we're not careful."

"She hasn't stopped talking about leaving since she got here. She wants a vacation fling."

"I don't think so. Even if that's what you think she thinks, you'll get attached."

"Sure, because there's no greater bonding experience than bondage and anal. Relax, Soren. This is fine."

I don't think it is fine. I think the moment we saw Aslin there's been something growing between us. It's more than attraction. It's more than antagonism. It's intense, and

Jason's given into it. But hey, we've got nothing to lose. Except, you know. Everything.

She stirs when I pick her up, then curls closer into my body. I feel a softening inside my chest, a warm welling of emotions I haven't felt in a long time. Jason and I didn't come to the depths of the jungle because we're good at relationships. We're equally terrible at them for different reasons. Yes, we've had women come and do the retreat before, and no, we haven't fucked them. From the moment Aslin got off the boat, she's broken all the rules. She shattered our professional boundaries the second she pushed Jason into the river; and the moment I put her over my knee, I think I was done.

I don't want to hurt her. Jason might be right. She might want to go home at the end of this. What am I thinking? Of course she wants to go home. She's not going to stay here; she's waiting for the supply boat because she hates us, and she hates being here, and... she makes a soft sound in her sleep and snuggles closer.

And I might fucking love her.

I know better than to let that thought go further than my own skull. She'd think I was crazy. Jason would laugh. But neither of those things stop my feelings from being what they are. She's beautiful. Absolutely stunning. She's bold, and she's brave, and she never, ever backs down.

"Are you going to put her down?"

"What?"

"You've been holding her for about an hour," Jason says, exaggerating.

I put her down on her bedroll and carefully tuck her in. She shifts a little in her sleep, but otherwise doesn't seem to wake.

"So you've got it bad, huh?"

"What?" I give Jason a glower that doesn't have any effect on him.

"You're in love."

"Oh, please," I say, immediately dismissing what I was just thinking about.

Jason knows me better than practically anybody on the planet. We've been through more together than I can list. Tours, missions, relationships. Since we were eighteen years old, we've had each other's backs. He's closer than a brother and lying to him won't work. I do it anyway.

He sighs. "Don't fall in love with her. She thinks she's too good for us. She thinks she's too good for anyone. That's why she's single."

"And why are we single?"

"Because we're the wrong kind of twisted and we scare the shit out of most girls, and the ones we don't scare don't want to live in the middle of nowhere. This girl is an executive or something."

"Or something? We should know that."

"I thought we did know that. It was on her application."

"Was it?"

I'm sure it was.

"How do we not know her better?" I ask the question to myself more than anything. It feels like we're acting on a serious lack of intel right now, and we both know better.

I know I have her application somewhere. I go to my little fireproof file box, the place I keep our passports, cash, and other documents of importance. Aslin's application is there. We don't actually read these as much as we wait to see if the check clears. I unfold the document, smooth it out on my thigh, and start reading.

"Aslin Reed," I say. "Hmmm uhmmm hmm..." I'm scanning for anything of interest. "The fuck?" I find myself swearing as I look up at Jason. "She declared herself to be a bank robber."

"She's not a bank robber," Jason laughs. Then he looks at me a little more seriously. "She's not a bank robber, is she?"

"She's got enough money to throw around, and she doesn't talk about a job. She doesn't really care how she spends it either, which people who have to earn their money usually do. And I've never heard her talk about owning property, which makes sense if all her gains are ill-gotten."

The laughter between us dies down a bit. I think it's pretty clear to us both with the way Aslin behaves, her complete disregard for rules, her refusal to bow to any kind of authority, and her absolute disinterest in consequences, she has all the markers of an adorably well-put-together little modern psychopath.

"It's late," Jason says. "We should get some rest before she runs us ragged tomorrow."

"Yeah," I agree. "Good idea."

I can't sleep. I'm worried. I'm worried that the money we've taken might be illegally sourced. I'm worried we might now be conspirators in the eyes of the law. I'm worried that she's done something very, very wrong. Most of all, I'm worried that I'm already deeply in love with her.

6

S *oren*

It's still dark when we get up. Usually we rise with the sun, but I don't think Jason or I slept well last night. It finally hit us that Aslin might not be more than she seems to be. She might be exactly what she seems to be.

Aslin stirs and looks over at us. The light from the fire plays over her face. There's so little innocence there, mischief dances in her eyes, a constant need to tease and taunt not just us, but the entire world. This is a woman who would defy a god if he would show himself to her.

"Hey," she says, rubbing her eyes. "What's going on?"

"Aslin," I say. "We checked your application last night. You put bank robber under occupation."

Aslin looks at me for a long moment, her dark eyes searching mine. laughs. "You really think I'm a bank robber!? Wow. Did you know the word gullible isn't in the dictionary?"

Aslin

Shit. I put the bank robber thing down as a joke. I'm not really a bank robber, of course. But I am, kinda. I'm not exactly the sort of person who makes a legal living, necessarily. When I filled out the form, I was drunk, and frankly, I didn't give a shit what the hell whoever read it thought. I guess I was pushing these two away before I even met them.

"So it was just another one of your little jokes. What is your profession, then?"

"I'm an internet celebrity. I make money posting pictures of myself online with filters that make my ass look huge, and my thighs look nonexistent. They call me Sticky."

Soren gives me a dark look. He's so serious. I think he really does suspect I'm a robber. What if I was? What's he going to do? Arrest me? He has no authority here.

"What's the big deal? What does it matter what I do? You haven't given a fuck who I was until now. You barely know me at all. Besides, maybe I'm an elementary school teacher who happened to come into an inheritance and decided to blow it on the retreat of a lifetime. You don't know."

"I'd like to know," he says. He's just so earnest. Goddammit.

"Serial fraudster," I say, straight faced. "I designed a program that steals the rounding errors from bank transactions, fractions of a penny at a time all adding up to millions of dollars."

Soren

"That's the plot of Office Space."

She is desperately avoiding the question. I am growing more and more suspicious with every passing minute. Or she's fucking with me, as usual. Dawn is starting to break, and with it the morning chorus of birdlife greeting the new day. It is too early to be wrapped up in her little games.

"Oh. Yeah," she grins. "Seriously, I'm in real estate. I sell expensive houses to rich assholes."

Why do I feel slightly disappointed at that answer? I know I didn't want her to secretly be a criminal, but a real estate agent? I don't see it for her. I don't think she has the ability to put her wilder impulses away for long enough to kiss ass.

"I'm going to fish us up some breakfast," she says. I think she wants this conversation to be over. I can tell by the way she moves back and forth on her bedroll that she's not comfortable. She grabs some clothes and scampers away as quickly as possible, like Jason and I are two inquisitors she needs to escape.

"I don't believe a single fucking word she said," Jason says, throwing his two pennies into the ring. "I don't know how she got her money, but I don't think she works for it. Heiress, maybe? Spoiled little rich girl?"

Spoiled little rich girl fits better than any explanation. Far better than bank robber. But guesses mean nothing.

"I'm going to send her details off to Brian. I want to know exactly who I am dealing with."

Brian is one of our contacts back in the States. He has access to every relevant database there is. I've yet to encounter someone he can't get complete data on. It's a point of pride and a major reason why he's so successful on the black market.

We have a radio that allows us to send brief messages through a relay, so I get the basic details sent. It's just a matter of waiting now. Soon I'll have all the information I could ever want or need on Aslin. I'll know where she grew up, where she went to school, how many siblings she has. I suppose I could just ask her those things, but there's something so satisfying about just knowing.

With that task done, I feel like I've done something useful, and that feeling gives me the sense of control I've lost touch with since Aslin arrived.

"I'm going to go talk to her," I tell Jason.

"Yeah, you are," he grins.

He knows I've got it bad for her. I'm not even going to try to deny it. My romantic impulses are twisted at the best of times, but she makes me want to be... normal.

Aslin is sitting on the dock wearing pink jeans and sneakers and a white tank top. Her shoulders are brown and one of the straps of the tank has moved slightly, showing a paler stripe of skin that looks incredibly sexy. I want her. I want her fucking bad. But I have more sense than Jason. I know better than to get involved with a stranger.

"Are the fish biting?"

"Not at the moment, but you never know when one will take the bait. Fishing teaches patience," she says, taking a swig from her little pink decanter, which I surmise does not contain water.

"I think you have a drinking problem, Aslin."

"I don't have a drinking problem. I just like to drink. Besides, I'm on vacation. Day drinking is part of the brief."

"You almost killed yourself diving into a river to get your booze back."

"That was about making a point."

"Uh huh. Still. Let's say no more drinking for a few days."

"Let's not."

I take the flask from her, expecting a tantrum. But Aslin just shrugs and starts reeling what might be her catch in. Her focus is on her prey, and mine is on her. I can't help but notice how expert she is, how she lets the fish run a bit before tightening up and drawing it in. She's letting it tire itself out, not risking the possibility that it will use all of its strength and break the line.

Before I know it, there's a fish on the hook and out of the water. Looks like a decent sized rainbow trout, a good fifteen pounds at least. The girl really knows how to handle a rod.

"Now that's breakfast," she declares, handing the beast over to me to dispatch and dress.

There's something about Aslin I just can't trust, something even more slippery than the trout, which makes a mighty thrashing motion as she walks past me and propels itself out of my hands and back into the water below, gone in an instant.

"Did that really just happen?" Her expression is a perfect mixture of judgement and amusement.

"Sorry," I say.

"Fumblefingers," she replies. "Guess I'll bait another hook."

She sits back down and does just that. She's not mad about me losing her fish at all. That's a good character trait, being patient. And kind. And having a great fucking sense of humor. And being absolutely adorable. And having that special spark, that wildness that usually gets beaten out of people early on.

I sit down next to her on the dock and watch her fish. There's a pleasant silence, a stillness of water moving and life happening.

"Tell me about where you grew up." I ask the question in the form of an order.

"Not much to tell. The great American wilderness, nothing to do but fish and hunt. Never liked hunting, but I did like fish, so I got used to fishing."

"You have brothers or sisters?"

She glances over at me, slightly perplexed. "I've got an older brother and an older sister. Both have different fathers and neither one of them lived with us. My mom raised me by herself out on the land. She used to milk a small herd of dairy cows for a local farmer."

"Sounds idyllic."

"Yeah. Well. Like most things that sound idyllic, it mostly smelled like shit."

She's cynical. I like that. I like everything about her, even the things I don't like.

"What about you?" She asks me back. "Where did you grow up?"

"Detroit."

"Really. Huh."

"Yep. Me and five brothers. My grandfather worked in the auto industry, my dad was unemployed, and I joined the military as soon as I could. Never looked back."

"That's why you're so straitlaced. Would have picked you for the rich boy, and Jason for the rough childhood."

"I didn't say I had a rough childhood."

"Did you?"

"A bit, yeah." I'm being vague. I don't want to go into my past right now. I want to learn about her.

"And what's Jason's deal? Black sheep, cast out of the family?"

"Close," I say. "But he can tell you his life story himself."

"Uh huh. I don't think he's the life story type. I don't think you are either," she says with a smart little smile on her lips, like she knows exactly what I am doing, fishing for information.

Out in the water, another unfortunate fish takes the bait. The float sinks, the reel unspools, and the drama unfolds once more with the same inevitable conclusion. In minutes, another trout dangles on her line. We're ready for breakfast.

7

A*slin*

Days go by, and I find myself increasingly on edge. It is not easy being out here. The environment is rough, and there's a lot of it. The fishing is good but avoiding Soren's increasing questions about my life and past is starting to take a toll.

It turns out that they're really serious about this no alcohol thing. I said I was fine, but I'm not fine. My mouth is dry, my head is pounding, and I'm starting to feel a little on edge too. Maybe I do have a drinking problem. Or maybe the hangover you get when you've been drinking since Kathmandu is not one you should let catch up with you.

Fortunately, my personal stash is not the only option. I remember the trail they tried to make me take to go up the hill. I also remember the turn off, and where that turn off goes. There's a village nearby, and I guarantee they've got something to drink.

So I sneak off one evening, right as Soren is getting water from the river, and Jason is trying to kill something with feet to break the constant stream of fish and rice we've been consuming of late. They've started to trust me, and I know this is going to put all that back to square one, but I'm okay with that. I don't owe them anything. It's my vacation. I'm the client. They should be grateful for the break.

I've prepared lightly, with a jacket, some US dollars and the sort of gumption you only get when you really want a drink. As I hustle out of camp, I look back over my shoulder every few seconds, but once I've gotten several hundred feet away, it occurs to me I'm going to get away with this.

The trail really isn't actually that bad. I might have been a bit dramatic when I refused to go up it. Sort of looks like it might be a nice wander. Anyway, that doesn't matter because I'm hanging a left to the local village.

The trees thin after a time, leaving me on the exposed lower slopes of what I can only describe as a fucking mountain. The track is narrow, more like a goat path than a real road. I guess the villagers don't use this route much. They must have another way down to the river.

It's a longer trek than I thought. It goes on, and on, and on, getting rockier and craggier, and as luck would have it, darker. I feel as though I can see some buildings in the distance, square shapes standing proud against the dying light, so I keep going. I am going to be hungry when I finally get there. I am guessing Tahr curry will be on the menu, given the prominence of the horned creatures stalking the heights above me.

This place is wild and untamed. It's remote, and I feel a certain thrill at being out here alone. This is what I need. Solitude. The kind of aloneness that reminds me who I am, and why I came here. I am a raft of secrets and misleads, half-truths and lies. Keeping my shit together with Jason and Soren is difficult, especially with the way Soren seems so very interested in getting under my skin. He wants more than I can give him. Though the wind is blowing increasingly cold across the mountains, and I am starting to wonder if I dressed for the conditions, I'm starting to think it's not a drink I needed. It was just some time alone.

S *oren*

"Where the fuck is Aslin?" Jason asks the question, annoyed. We left her to wash the rice and put it over the fire, but she seems to have taken the opportunity to disappear instead. I'd like to say I'm surprised, but nothing she does surprises me now. I check the riverbank. That's usually where she is. She's not there, and the light is starting to fade.

"Do you think she went for a walk?"

"Why would she go for a walk?"

I think about that for a second, which is all it takes to come up with the obvious answer. "To get a drink. Remember. We told her about the village."

"But it's above the snow line. She'll freeze if she tries to get there tonight. Or she'll get eaten. Did we not give her the orientation? Did we not tell her about the fucking tigers?"

"No. We didn't. She pushed you in the river and we forgot all about orientation. We've been trying to keep up with her this entire time."

"For fuck's sake," Jason curses. He's staring at me with an annoyed expression bordering on the stunned. "How can one person be this much fucking trouble?"

"She doesn't seem to care what happens to her," I say. "It's almost like she wants to get hurt, or she thinks she can't get hurt."

"She's going to learn otherwise up there," he says.

As we talk, we're gathering supplies for a rescue. There's a chance that she's already seriously hurt. The village is located high on the mountain, built as a sort of mountain pass fortress. It's a strategic location, not a vacation destination.

I am angry at her. Furious. With all the bullshit she's pulled since she got here, I shouldn't be surprised. But this is going a step too far. Being a brat, sneaking liquor, swimming defiantly, fine. But going up into the mountains in light clothing at night basically reflects a death wish.

"What's wrong with her?" I growl the question as we set out.

"You know exactly what's wrong with her. No fucking discipline. No common sense. No understanding that anything bad can happen to her. She's like a goddamn baby."

Jason is also angry. It's hard not to be. She seemed to have common sense, to be someone who knew how to take care of themselves or at least not make outright suicidal decisions out here in the wild. There is no reason whatsoever to go up a mountain to a village you've been told is 'somewhere'. It is madness. It's stupid. Aslin's not stupid. Or at least, I had hoped she wasn't. I thought she was smart. I'm disappointed in her, and I'm scared that we're already too late. If the weather turns bad up there, with what she was wearing...

"This terrain creeps me the fuck out," Jason curses. We both have good reason to be wary of rocky mountain passes in low light. Past experience has taught us they're bad places to be pinned down, and worse places to be pulled out of.

*Y*ears ago...

Jason and I are moving up the side of a mountain on a cool night. It's a relief from the relentless heat of the day. There's a target we need to reach a few miles up, and we're making good progress.

Thwip.

I hear a whisper, and then I feel an ache propelling me toward the side of the mountain. Being shot is less dramatic than people think it is. I collapse, grabbing above my knee. There's a sniper somewhere on the opposing range, tucked into the shadows, sending missives of death toward me with near devastating accuracy.

Being hit is always a shock. You know it can happen, but it's still very strange when it does happen. My leg is warm and doesn't want to work. I don't know if he hit bone, but the amount of blood I'm trying to staunch tells me he at least nicked an artery.

Another bullet ricochets off a nearby rock. Two shots. A trained sniper would move at this point, but he's local and there's very little chance of returning fire accurately. He can sit there and take shots for as long as it takes to kill me.

Jason's by my side before I utter a word. He drags me behind a rock and tourniquets my leg. He works fast, and he says very little. He and I are close to strangers, two soldiers chosen because we have prior experience in this kind of operation. He saves my life in seconds.

BOOM!

A bullet makes very little noise. An RPG makes a fuckton of sound. It throws up dust and dirt and turns small stones into shrapnel. The rock we're hiding behind has developed a deep crack. It won't withstand another hit. These guys have gotten very good with their stolen weaponry, looted from abandoned camps and turned against its makers.

Jason looks at me and smirks. He's covered in filth, and an arc of blood across his cheek makes me think he's been cut. Then he wipes it away, and I realize it was my blood.

"We should get out of here," he says casually, like we're at a movie that sucks. "Can you walk?"

I can't walk. But I can stumble and slide on the shale, and roll and move with every little bit of help gravity can give me. Jason helps me up and propels me onward when he can, half dragging, half carrying, half chasing me as we tumble down the mountain with RPG shells landing around us. The sniper can't get a bead on us amid the moonlit dust, but that doesn't stop him from taking potshots at us until we finally reach the tree line.

· · ·

*T*onight...

My leg still aches on nights like this. It's not the weather. It's not anything physical at all. It's my body desperately trying to tell me to stay fucking clear of this kind of terrain.

"You okay?" Jason asks the question casually.

"Fine," I say. I'm not fine. I'm angry, and I'm scared for Aslin. There are no snipers up here, but there are tigers and crevasses. There's cold and wind, and those last two factors alone can be lethal, especially now that it is starting to spit. The weather can change in a second on this mountain range, and rarely for the better.

"Do we assume she stayed on the path? Or do you think she just wandered somewhere?"

"I have no idea. The path isn't exactly well marked. Did she think the village was up high? Or did she think she just needed to go more or less straight?"

"If you have any idea what she thinks, you're ahead of me. Girl makes no damn sense," Jason says. We're scanning the mountainside with binoculars and night vision. The potential area is vast, especially if she fell. It's easy to twist an ankle on loose rock or encounter a prowling animal. There are tigers in these regions, but it's not just tigers we need to watch out for. Mountain lions prowl this terrain, and they have been opportunistic before.

Aslin is not prepared to face the reality of the wild. She's a snack for any predator who chances across her path and smells her particular brand of delicious femaleness. Which brings me to another possibility, bandits. People don't think of bandits as a modern-day issue, but with villages dotted across mountains and valleys, and people traveling between them with wares mostly held on their backs or on the backs of beasts of burden, the opportunity for theft is irresistible to some.

"ASLIN!" I shout her name to the wind. It is carried a little distance before being carried back to me on the waking wind. It is starting to blow more heavily now, little shards of icy water being whipped against our faces. The wind chill factor is only going to increase.

"BRAT!" Jason calls out.

That brings a hint of a smile to my lips, but just a hint. This is bad. This is Very. Very. Bad. If we don't find her soon, the weather could close in so bad we have no chance of finding her at all. Her chances of surviving without shelter out here overnight are basically nil. I am forced to face the fact that we might have lost her forever. It's not a useful thought, but I carry it with me every step of the way.

Jason

Absolute little shit. I am going to beat her ass when I find her. She's not leaving our sight again, that's for sure. Soren and I need about three other guys to keep track of her. That's what happens when you're dealing with a complete rogue. I've known from the first moment Aslin pushed me into the river she was going to be a handful, and I doubt this'll be the last curveball she throws us. As long as she's around, we're going to be living life on high alert.

I see Soren stumble a fraction. It's his fucking leg. He says it doesn't hurt, but we both have scars, seen and unseen from our service. We figured starting this remote boot camp vacation would allow us to make good money, not have to deal with too many people, and avoid the society neither one of us really fits in with anymore.

Aslin fits with us in a way most people don't. Yes, she's a little shit. Yes, she's a liar. No, I don't trust her at all, but when she's around the camp it feels more like home than it ever has before. I can't quite put my finger on what it is that makes her feel like ours, but I think she might be ours.

"Is that smoke?"

I point toward an outcrop of rocks. Soren doesn't say anything. He just starts running toward it. His leg doesn't seem to hurt anymore. He runs like a gazelle. Long legs. Powerful strides. He recovered from his wounds well. All of them. We both did. At least, we can pretend we did at times like these.

There is smoke. I'm afraid it's from a local trader or some other source, but a pink piece of fabric flutters over the outcropping. It's Aslin. I'm sure of it. Soren's shout of joy assures me.

Aslin used rocks to turn her windbreaker into a tent roof and started a fire with what was at hand, which was some moss, a bundle of hundred dollar bills, and her shoe. The shoe was actually a good idea. Made a nasty black smoke you couldn't help seeing.

She wipes a tear off her cheek and forces a smile at us. "Hey, guys," she says. "What are you doing out here?"

"Aslin!"

"You guys definitely didn't mention the terrible weather on the website," she says. "Also, I think something tried to eat me. I had to wave a fiery stick at it, and it went away, but it might be back."

"Aslin!" Soren grabs her and holds her close, crouching to hold her against the rocks near the remnants of her fire. That thing would not have lasted much longer, but she's done fucking well to set up so much camp with so little. That's what connects us all. We're survivors.

"Aslin, why?" Soren's voice cracks as he asks the question. I can't hear if she responds. The wind has started to shriek and squall as the weather turns worse and worse. We could go back down to camp but trying to traverse this terrain in the wet is asking for broken bones and maybe broken necks.

"I reckon we set up here," Soren says. I nod in agreement.

We have come prepared. We have a tent designed to withstand high winds, and we have warming packs and foil blankets. We have sleeping bags, and we have food. It's going to be a tight, intimate fit, but we're going to make it.

S*oren*

Aslin wipes her eyes and her nose. She's been sniffling and perhaps crying for a long time. Thick tears have traced lines down the windblown dust clinging to her face. Having her in my arms, I feel pure relief. I feel as though I was just handed back the most important thing in the world. She's shivering against me, though I do not think she is cold anymore. I think she's in shock.

She looks small and scared, and all the anger I felt when I realized what she did has quieted for the moment. We found her. Fate has been kinder than she, or we, deserve. I can't stop remembering how she looked when I came around the corner. Aslin was there, curled up against the rocks, knees up to her chin, arms wrapped around her legs. The wind was whipping around her loudly enough that she didn't hear us coming. She was tucked up in herself, a little pink bundle of misery waiting for the elements to take her.

Now we have the tent up, and Aslin tucked up inside it, wearing a sleeping bag and wrapped with air activated heat packs. She's looking better already, though she's still cold and scared.

"You need to eat," I tell her. "And you're going to."

"Yes, sir," she says. She's never called me sir before, and I don't know if she ever will again, but for this small moment, it's quite sweet. I think she knows how big of a mistake she made, and how much trouble she is in.

"Never thought I'd be happy to see one of these," she says ruefully, taking the MRE from me. "I'm sorry I dragged you guys up here. I really didn't mean to put you in danger. I just had to get away."

There's something haunting about the way those words come out of her mouth. It's like it's not a simple apology. There's a weight to the words, a meaning I don't think we understand.

"What did you have to get away from?" I activate her heat pack for her. Her fingers are shaking too much to do it for herself.

She shakes her head, wordlessly. I can feel something between us. Something lurking beneath the surface of her skin, hiding behind her dark eyes. It almost surfaced for a moment, but it is gone again. I feel a deep sadness, some of it mine, but most of it hers. There is so much pain in this girl, so much that has gone unsaid, perhaps forever.

"Aslin. I'm here for you."

"I'm a client," she reminds me. "I'm a pain in the ass client. You don't need to be here for me, you've just got to survive until the supply boat comes and then you can be rid of me."

"I don't want to be rid of you."

"Soren, now's not the time," Jason says. He's right. This is not a moment to have deep conversations. Aslin is barely alive, and we all have to focus on surviving the night.

"I'm sorry," she repeats. "I'll be gone soon."

Her teeth are chattering. Her shock is getting worse. Jason wraps another foil blanket around her and breaks out the warming packs, but he's shaking his head as he does it.

"We should get in with you. There's only so much these packs can do. Two bodies produce a lot more energy than a few of these packs."

A*slin*

I nod. I am cold. More than cold, I'm frozen to my core. It's not just a matter of temperature. I came all the way up here to try to get away, and all I ended up discovering was that my biggest problem was still there. Me. I am my greatest enemy, and I'm never going to be able to escape me.

They are disrobing. Not completely. They are taking their outer clothing off, stripping down to their thermal underwear. They join the sleeping bags together and put me in the middle, two sets of arms wrapped around me, two bodies pressed against mine, two strong, masculine forms keeping me safe against the dangers of the night.

I wonder why they haven't sought out partners. Why aren't they living normal lives with wives and kids? Why do they seek this isolation and rush so gladly to the dark, cold night? To me, Soren and Jason seem like the most stable, even-handed people I have ever met. But my perceptions are skewed. I come from chaos, and so do they. We are two sides of the same coin. We are different flavors of the same ice cream. We are...

8

Morning has come and the weather has cleared. Bright sun greets me, as does the smell of an egg burrito that has been inside a ration pack for months. It smells fucking delicious.

"Yum," I say, grabbing at the food. It happens to have been in Soren's hand a moment ago, but my hunger demands that I take it.

"What the hell do you think you're doing?"

I take a bite and hand it back. "Morning. Where's Jason?"

"Taking a piss," Jason shouts from outside the tent.

That sounds like a good idea to me. I need to pee. I need to eat. And I need for Soren to stop glaring at me.

S *oren*

She's not sorry anymore. The submissive, sad little girl we found last night has returned to the self-assured, arrogant, brat of a woman. I'm half-glad I was able to see her as she was last night, but I am not glad how it happened, or not knowing why.

"You have no shoe," I tell her. "So we're going to carry you back down today. After what you did last night, consider yourself in trouble of the most extreme and intense kind."

Her face falls a little. She was expecting the softer man from last night as well, the one who held her while the storm raged. But he has gone too, replaced by the commanding officer who is going to tear strips off his disobedient subordinate. The way she woke up, grinning, cheerful, absolutely without any kind of remorse, that's not going to fly. I'm going to make her sorry. I'm going to make her small. And I'm going to discover her secret.

"Let's get this shit broken down and get back to the camp," Jason says, throwing back the tent awning. "Get dressed, Aslin. We're taking you home."

"Not my home," she says. "Your home, though? Why do you guys live so far out? It can't be for the company, spoiled rich people who think the whole thing is a joke."

"Most people aren't as rude as you," I say. "Or as trying. Most people take what we do seriously. Most people take themselves and their lives more seriously."

Aslin

Here come the lectures. I knew that once we were all safe I was going to be in trouble. I just didn't think I'd be in this much trouble this quickly. Last night I felt bad. This morning I feel a lot better. In the light of day it is easy to pretend that the actions of the evening were a specific and unique kind of madness. I'm not the same person I was last night, right? And Soren's making too much of this, right?

"You woke up on the wrong side of the bed," I pout.

He reaches out and grabs me by the back of the head, suddenly. His fingers fist in my hair and he uses the grasp to pull me hard up against him, our noses touching.

"I woke up knowing that you need to be handled differently," he says. "You wait until I get you home, young lady."

Fuck me. A thrill runs right through to the core of me. Is he trying to turn me on? I don't think so. The way his eyes flash at me tells me he's really angry. I've pissed this guy off. I have managed to push him beyond the kind limits of what he wants to be.

I grab his burrito, and I shove it right into my mouth. If he's going to beat me, I need to be fed.

He glares at me. I chew. He glares at me harder. I chew more.

"What?" I ask the question through a mouthful, which is not ladylike, but hey. I have limited options here, and I am starving.

"Do you really think you can get out of this by stealing my breakfast?" His grip tightens on my hair. "You're..." He stops talking, lost for words. "You're incorrigible."

I finish his burrito.

"Jason," he says. "Come get this girl."

Jason comes in. He's fully dressed and ready to go. He reaches for me, grabs my arm, and slings me up over his shoulder like a spider monkey. The way he handles me makes me feel so very small and feminine. He's just so strong, and unlike Soren, he doesn't seem to be simmering with barely suppressed rage.

"Alright, let's get you back," he says.

Soren finishes packing up the camp behind us while Jason starts carrying me down.

"Are you mad at me?" I ask the question in his ear.

"Always," Jason grunts. "Quiet down back there. You're not getting out of trouble any time soon."

"Okay. Sure. You're mad at me, but are you, you know, mad at me? The way Soren is? Because Soren's really angry."

"Yeah, he is. You should worry less about him being angry, and more about your tendency to do stupid shit that will get you killed one of these days. You got a death wish or something?"

"No. I don't have a death wish. I just need to..."

"Get away. Yeah. You've said that more than once. Most people think about what they're doing before they do it. You just do things."

"I think sometimes," I say. "Yesterday, no. Not a great example, but in general I'm pretty good at planning. I'm not as stupid as you think. I'm not always burning shoes to chase tigers away."

We're back inside the trees now. It's a lot warmer here, and more sheltered. I guess the forest and the river help moderate temperatures. Geography, or whatever.

"I really thought you'd be the angry one," I pipe up again.

"I am angry, but Soren is something much worse."

"What's that?"

"He's disappointed."

"Oh, fuck," I almost laugh. "You're talking like he's my father."

"Not your father," Jason mutters. "Maybe your daddy."

"What?"

"Nothing. Listen, for the rest of the day, you're going to lay low, get some rest, and stay out of his way. Trust me when I tell you this is not something you want to deal with today. Soren doesn't get angry quick, and he doesn't calm down quickly either. That cutesy shit with the burrito? You're going to need to cut that shit out."

We're back at camp now. Jason deposits me next to my bags, where I have a few spare pairs of shoes. I'm going to be able to sort my feet out now, but that's the least of my worries.

"I am sorry, Jason," I say. "Really. If I do something that dumb again you don't have to come after me. Just let me get what I deserve."

"Self-pity is not going to help now," he says. "You want to show us you're sorry? Do as you're told, get some rest, and stay out of the way — but in sight. Got it?"

"Yes! I got it!"

Soren is back not long after we arrive. He comes downhill lugging the baggage. He doesn't even look at me as he dumps his load. He stashes his stuff and starts ordering it without saying a word. I'm tempted to say something, but he doesn't say anything, and I remember what Jason said about being quiet.

I can actually behave myself, believe it or not. Especially when I'm feeling this bad. They saved me. They took care of me. This morning, first thing, with the burrito, I thought I might be able to charm my way out of the situation. But I don't think I can.

It's obvious that he's disappointed in me. He's furious with me. Still. Even after a long night's sleep. I thought by morning he would be willing to forgive me, to hug me and tell me he's glad I am okay.

"We're going to meditate now," Jason tells me.

Usually I'd refuse, but today I think better of opening my mouth and telling them what I think. I take my place on the dock and sit between them, and I try not to get into any more trouble. Jason's usually somewhere on the spectrum of pissed the hell off, but Soren is always softer, kinder. Not today, though. Today I sit between two masculine pillars of stoic annoyance, and I feel smaller and increasingly more guilty with every deep breath I take.

When it's over, they get up and go about the tasks of the morning, putting water to boil, chopping wood for the fire. Nobody says anything to me. It's like I've been shut out. I hate this. I hate this more than any other punishment they've given me. It's not that they're completely ignoring me, it's just that there's no kind attention, no softer looks, no intimacy of any kind. It's hard to believe they cuddled me all night long. Though I guess it wasn't really a cuddle. It was an attempt to keep me, and themselves, alive.

Lunch happens. And then the afternoon drags on by, with nothing to do, and nobody talking to me still, at least, not unless they need to.

"Soren?" I eventually approach him. I can't stand it any longer. I will take any kind of treatment over this lack of interaction. "Are you ever going to talk to me again?"

He turns to me and looks down at me with those hard blue eyes that are usually not hard at all. "You want to do this now?"

"Yes. Please."

He reaches around me and grabs me by the scruff of my neck. That grip is becoming familiar. And hot. His touch alone fills me with hope that I might soon be forgiven after all.

"Then let's deal with it," he says, pulling me to the camp, to the very center of the gazebo. Jason is nearby, but not interfering. This is between Soren and me, and I am sensing an intensity that has not been there before. I pushed him too far this time. I made him too angry. I wish I knew how to make men not angry, but my talents lie entirely in the other direction.

"What you did yesterday was reckless, dangerous, and borderline suicidal," he says. Lectures, really? I know I deserve this, but it is so hard to take. "We thought you were dead."

"But I wasn't. You should be pleased. Not furious."

"You're a bad little girl," he growls. "An absolute spoiled brat with no conscience and no consideration for anybody who cares about you."

He's really fucking mad. It's not that he's angry out of professional concern. He's, like, personally angry. I have pissed him the fuck off with this little stunt, and he's probably more convinced than ever that I have a drinking problem. So I do what I always do when I'm in the wrong: I get defensive.

"What do you care? I'm a client. You hardly know me, and I don't owe you obedience. I thought I made that clear from the outset."

"You did. Now it's time for me to make something very clear. You do owe me obedience, because I just clambered up a mountain in the dark searching for you, hoping not to find you with your neck broken. You owe me because I've pledged to keep you safe."

"Yeah? What are you going to do? Spank me? Fuck my ass? What sexual perversion are you going to indulge in to make up for my naughty behavior, *sir*...?"

I throw the *sir* in with an extra lilt. He seemed to like that the first time I said it.

Soren's eyes flare with anger. "You could have died. Don't you understand? You put yourself in lethal danger just to get a drink. You're not this stupid, are you?"

"I might be this stupid, you don't know."

It's not the best comeback. I am feeling guilty. Really fucking guilty. I already knew I'd done something very stupid when the trees went away. It's a bad sign when even trees don't want to go where you're going. But I kept on because I'm not a quitter, and because the wilderness gave me some sense of peace.

"You're a very bad little girl," he growls again. "And no, I'm not going to spank you right now, or fuck your ass. You don't deserve to have any of your holes fucked." God. He's being crude. Is there anything hotter than a straitlaced guy finally getting filthy?

"I'm going to ground you. You're not going anywhere. Understand? You're going to stay in my sight at all times, and you are going to do as you are told without question. If you disobey me, you'll be punished. Hard."

Crude and paternalistic at the same time. I don't know what to do with those two things. I'm scared, turned on, and of course offended, but there's no point getting offended. Everything about the way they treat me is offensive and patriarchal. Maybe I deserve it. Maybe I need it.

Soren grabs me again and puts me on my knees. That's where he likes me when I am being lectured. That's probably how he wants me all the time. On my knees, looking up at him, mouth at cock height, vulnerable, obedient, submissive.

"Stay."

He snaps the order at me like I'm a dog.

"What is this..."

I feel him looping something around my neck, a smooth circle of leather that buckles at the back. A collar.

"What do we do with bad little pups who can't be trusted not to run away?"

"I have no fucking idea."

"We chain them," he says. "You're not leaving this area."

I didn't even notice the chain. I mean, I did, but I didn't notice it was actually attached to me. It's linked to the D ring at the rear of the collar, and it gives him extra leverage over me and my faithless little neck.

I could just take the collar off, if I wanted. Something in Soren's eye tells me that would be a mistake. It's like I triggered something in him, pushed aside the bookcase of propriety hiding his inner secret passage of all kinds of fucked up.

I'm curious. I shouldn't be, but I am. I wonder how far he's going to go with this chain thing, and what else lurks behind those suddenly dark blue eyes.

He might be angry with me, but it's not the kind of angry that makes people turn away. It's the kind that shows the obsession that's been lurking inside him since we met. Soren wants me, and now he's going to take me.

He tugs on the chain, wrapping it around his fist. His teeth are gritted, his eyes lit with need. I can see his cock straining at his pants. He's turned the fuck on. And so am I.

"You don't need to make this worse for yourself this time," he says. "What I'm going to do to you will push the limits you understand for yourself. I am going to make you regret your disobedience."

He turns me around with my back against his stomach and spreads my legs, his hand sliding down between my breasts, over my stomach, the hard, muscular lines of his strong arm rippling as his fingers curl around my mound and squeeze. He plays with me over my panties. They are a silky blend, and he pulls them tighter over my clit and slit and his fingers run down over those same delicate places. He's not rough like Jason, but he is an absolute master of the female form. He begins lightly, but still completely in control. He rubs the tips of his fingers in a circle around my clit until I am moaning and squirming my hips. He keeps the collar tight, not tight enough to cut breath from my lungs, but tight enough to let me know I am owned. This collar is more than a dirty sex toy. It is a symbol of his control and of my submission, however reluctant.

My first climax is small and could almost be denied, but the second is more intense, and the third follows quickly. I am soaking my underwear, until he decides to pull it to the side, and I finally feel the heat of his fingers against my bare pussy. I am slick with my juices, and I am swollen and desperate. I don't know if I want him to stop, or if I want him to finally fuck me.

He doesn't stop.

And he doesn't fuck me.

Before I know it, I am screaming in orgasm, time and time again as his fingers rub, slap, tease and pinch my sensitive clit and lips until I come, and come again. Orgasm has become something quite other than pleasure. It has become a punishment, one I know I deserve.

"Tell me what you want," he growls in my ear. I am whimpering and barely coherent. I am writhing, and when I look down at myself I see his hand and the soft, wet, spread lips of my sex, the dirty bud of my clit. I see my need. I smell it. And I need him to give me what he has made me crave so desperately.

"I need you to fuck me, please."

I have never asked so nicely before. I have never been made so very polite.

He lifts me up under my arms and pushes me up onto my knees, and then over again, face down, ass up. The most animal position you can be fucked in. He makes me wait, wet and spanked. Punished, and pleasured. He makes me feel the full force of my submission to him, how much I want to please him even though I don't really know how.

Then, finally, I feel his cock. I need him so badly. I need his dick more than I can say. I've been craving this and fearing this from the moment we first met. The sensation of bare, hot flesh against my pussy makes me clench with anticipation. Is he going to do it? I want him to do it. I...

"Ohh!" I let out a long sigh as he gives me what I've been craving, his thick cock deep inside me in one long, possessive stroke.

He has me on hands and knees, the collar working against my throat, my ass arched up toward his plunging cock. I'm soaked. I can feel it, and I can hear it. My wet shame is clear to everyone in earshot. And there is someone in earshot. Someone coming over to us now. Someone with dark eyes and a huge...

Jason cups my chin in his hand and looks deep into my eyes as Soren punishes my pussy with rough, disciplinary thrusts. There's no escaping this sexual shame. His eye contact alone intensifies the moment, making me feel great waves of pleasure rushing through me. Is it pleasure, though? Or is it just the sheer energy of being caught between two sexy military beasts, of fucking and being fucked, of being at their absolute mercy and use.

Jason kneels up before me and frees his cock from his pants. His cock is as I remember it, heavy and thick and imposing. The kind of rod designed to not just fuck a girl but teach her a lesson.

He pushes inside my mouth, that cock sliding over my tongue with a possessive and yes, punishing stroke. He fills my mouth completely, his hand still under my jaw, keeping me in place, giving me exactly what I deserve.

Soren is pounding my pussy harder and faster, his big hands curling in my hair. They're both gripping my head, both trying to control the one thing they can never control: my mind. They can use my body, but they don't know me. They can't claim what lies at the core of me. But they can make my body shake and quiver, they can make lewd sounds emerge from both ends. They can shame, humiliate, and claim my flesh, and I will let them, because the pleasure that coils along my spine, makes my toes curl, and takes me out of my body entirely is absolutely worth it.

I scream in orgasm as Soren floods my pussy with his seed. My lips and tongue lap and contort around Jason's cock and send him over that invisible edge we have all been desperately trying to reach since this began.

He comes. I come. Soren comes. Soren's cock throbs inside my ravaged little cunt, pulsing and filling me with that great big muscular rod. His seed spills from me when he pulls free, and then is pushed deeper inside me when he drives back in again. It's not enough to fuck me, or to come inside me. He has to drive it in again and again. He is using his cock to spread his seed around my pussy, to make it sink into every part of me, to mark me as his.

Afterward, he holds me. He holds the chain in his hands, and I turn my face up to him. I let him see me, as much of me as can safely be seen, and I ask the question that has been burning inside me.

"Do you forgive me?"

"You're forgiven," Soren says. "But don't make any mistake, Aslin. The rules have changed. You're my pup now. You belong to me, and you do as I say."

You belong to me. Those words stick in my mind and play themselves over and over again. They make me feel warm, and loved, or maybe something more than loved. Possessed. Safe. Held. His. *Theirs.*

I finally fall asleep, and properly this time, not the broken sleep I got last night that was shallow from guilt. This is the deep kind of sleep that only the forgiven can experience, wrapped in the arms of someone I can feel cherishes me.

9

S *oren*

"Feel better?"

"Much," I answer Jason.

Aslin is still asleep next to us, exhausted and finally, maybe, under control. We fucked for most of the evening, and then we all slept together again last night in a big pile of sexually satiated limbs. I was warm and I was happy. I felt like I'd finally gotten through to her, and that maybe we'd made a connection that would finally lead to the truth.

He grins. It was never really a question in either of our minds that we would share Aslin. She's too much trouble for any one man to handle. I was hesitant, thinking she might be too delicate — though I knew she wasn't delicate. I am ashamed, to some extent, of my appetites. It takes a special woman to withstand my love, and an even more rare one to blossom in it. I think I've known from the beginning that Aslin was for me, but I couldn't be sure until it happened.

"Do you know exactly what you have on your leash? You think it's a puppy, but it might turn out to be a panther cub."

Jason is still grinning.

"You think she's a bank robber?"

"I think she's..." He shakes his head. "I think she's a survivor. That can mean a lot of things. When people have to learn how to get by, they usually learn a lot of other dangerous things besides. I have to wonder how much she's been hurt."

As luck would have it, we don't have to speculate too much longer. When we check the comms equipment, there's a message waiting for us, a blinking light on the radio indicating something is ready to be downloaded. Bill left me a message about Aslin. Finally, the mystery is going to be resolved, or we'll at least know a little more about her.

"**A**slin Reed doesn't exist," Brian's voice says, crackly and gravelly. In the early morning light, it's a creepy missive to receive. "There's no record of any Aslin Reed existing before about six months ago. I don't know who you have out there but be careful."

"Well. Fuck," Jason curses.

"She might have a good reason to be using a fake name." I leap immediately to the best possible interpretation of the facts. "A lot of women have to change their names when they leave bad relationships."

"And she's obviously hiding out here," Jason adds.

"So we can assume there's an ex somewhere in the picture," I murmur.

"We might have to actually talk to her," Jason says.

"If she is up to something criminal, she's not going to tell us. And, given how close she likes to play things to the vest, she might not tell us if there's an ex, either."

"Might not be an ex," Jason says.

We don't have time to explore that idea because suddenly we are hearing the thrum of a motor coming up the river. That's odd. There's no reason for it to be coming.

"Boat is coming a week early?" Jason frowns. "What's going on?"

We walk down to the riverbank together. Once glance down tells us we're in trouble. The boat is not being driven by a local. And it is not being crewed by locals. There are at least six heavily-armed men aboard, wearing tactical clothing. It's a raiding party.

We run back to camp, where Aslin has made herself scarce. We don't have time to find her right now, and by the looks of things she knows better than to come out.

"This has something to do with her," Jason says, stating the obvious. Our world has revolved around Aslin from the moment we met her, chaos unfolding at an ever increasing rate. Every time we think we have a line on her, everything spins out again.

The floor of the camp rotunda comes up to reveal a cache of weapons and ammunition, all carefully wrapped in oilskins.

We're ready for any eventuality. We have to be. When you're this far from civilization the law becomes more of a suggestion than something set in stone.

We're prepared to defend ourselves. Aslin is still scarce, and that indicates to me she knows what's going on here. Our instincts were correct. She comes with more than baggage. She comes with men with guns. Two sets of them. Them and us, as it turns out.

We go back down to the dock, where the boat is already making land. The invading force believes that they have the advantage, being more numerous, but our guns work as well as theirs and nobody came here wanting to be shot. We keep our barrels diagonal and down, and I greet them.

"How can we help you, gentlemen?"

No point starting with aggression. There's plenty of that latent in this altercation already.

It's Jason who ends up breaking the tension.

"Barry? Barry Wozniak? Is that you?"

A man on the other side of the armed line lifts his visor. "Jason?"

"Barry!" Jason repeats his name. "How the hell are you, man?"

"Oh, not bad, working the mercenary rounds, you know."

The leader, a man with a thick Jersey accent interjects. "Where's the bitch?"

Jason and I exchange looks. We know who he is referring to, but decorum states we don't let armed men talk about Aslin that way.

"Who?"

"This bitch." He holds up a piece of paper with Aslin's face printed on it. She looks a little different. Her hair is blonde and she's wearing a lot of makeup, but it's definitely her.

"Who is that?" Jason asks. He plays dumb more competently than anybody would ever suspect.

"You seen her, or not?"

"No. We haven't seen her."

"Our intel suggests she came here."

"We had a client booked, but she never showed. Don't know what she looked like, but she paid a nonrefundable deposit. What's her name? And what agency are you boys with?"

We all know this group of assholes isn't with any agency, but plenty of them are ex-military. They don't want to shoot us any more than we want to shoot them. We've all seen more than enough blood for a lifetime, is my guess.

"Aslin Reed, or Ash White," the leader of the unit says. "And probably half a dozen different other names. She's wanted by Luca Vitori."

We all know what that means. The Vitori name is synonymous with organized crime, and excellent dining. I didn't know he sent kill squads to distant nations, but mercs gotta merc. There are more actions undertaken by private armies in the world than anybody suspects.

"These guys are legit," Barry says. "I've done tours with Jason, and I know Soren by reputation. They don't want trouble."

That's a polite way of saying they don't want to make trouble with us.

"So this Aslin, what's she done? Doesn't look like the type to normally be the target of this kind of operation."

"None of your fuckin' business."

"Sorry," I say. "Didn't catch your name."

"You can call me Big Dick," he says. "Let us know if the girl shows."

"Really? Big Dick? That name doesn't suit you," Jason says. "No, you're more like an Asshole."

Big Dick reaches for his side arm.

"Don't." Jason steps forward. His gun's not raised, and nor is mine, but the tension is hitting a dangerous point. Big Dick wants to dominate the situation. He has no military training. He's a thug with a bunch of paid mercenaries behind him, and I'd put money on it that every single one of them would rather put a bullet in him than us. Is he self-aware enough to know that? I'm guessing not.

"We'd like to know who we are dealing with, and why," I say. "You'd be doing us a courtesy if there's a criminal coming. It would be good to know what sort of person we made a booking with."

"She's a thief."

Jason and I glance at each other. Sounds like she stole from Luca Vitori, which seems unlikely, even given her penchant for terrible decisions.

"Well, she's not here," I say. "As I said, the booking was made, but nobody ever showed."

Barry steps forward, further attempting to defuse the situation. "She could be anywhere. Signed up for five different vacations from here to Antarctica," he says. "Smart cookie."

Big Dick feels otherwise. The string of curses that emits from his lips is quite spectacular. He doesn't think she's a smart cookie. He thinks she's a bitch who deserves to die. There's something personally aggrieved in his approach. I wonder if he was one of the weak links in the chain she exploited.

"Let's go," he says. "We'll find the little cunt. Don't think we won't. Luca Vitori is going to get his money back, and she's going to get what she deserves."

"Alright. Well. We have an elderly tour group booked in a day or so, they'll be in to learn about survival, so keep an eye out for some geriatrics wobbling about the place. They tend to spook easy and make complaints."

I am lying because I know they don't want to deal with normal people. People who will take real offense to their luxury adventure holidays being interrupted by armed men. People who will talk and be missed by loving children and grandchildren. People who will make a mess.

"Yeah, we'll leave the Disney tours to you boys," Big Dick says. Barry gives us an apologetic wave and they file back onto their hired boat, and they putt off back down the river toward the village. They're way too close for comfort, but at least they're gone. Probably. We need to sweep for scouts. If it were me, I would have dropped a man nearby to keep a covert eye on things, make initial contact, and then pretend to leave. Best way to flush a fugitive out is to make them feel like they've gotten clear.

Jason and I walk and wait long enough to make sure that doesn't happen, following the boat back downriver to ensure that there are no drop-offs. We can't ensure they don't come back, or that they didn't already drop a spy, but it's the best we can do for now, and it gives us time to think.

"We were warned," Jason says on the walk back.

"Yes. We were." Bill's limitations stop with the law. He can tell me if someone has active warrants or previous interaction with authorities. He can't tell me if the person I'm inquiring about is mixed up with outlaws if they haven't been under scrutiny.

The only saving grace is that Aslin has the sense to make herself properly scarce. She's so good at it that it takes several hours for her to emerge, which, on the heels of her last little excursion, has not put either one of us in a good mood.

The light is almost completely gone when Aslin emerges sheepishly from the undergrowth, still wearing the collar I put on her neck. It looks a little outlandish now, because the notion of collaring someone like Aslin is like trying to chain the wind. No sooner do I think I've gotten her under control than she turns even wilder.

"Where the fuck have you been?" Jason growls the question. Aslin already has her palms lifted in a placating measure, like that's going to make this alright.

"Okay. So. Guys. You're probably going to be angry about this, but I figure I should tell you. There are some people who are coming after me due to a misunderstanding."

"What kind of misunderstanding?"

Her eyes dart around in a way that makes me think whatever comes after that look is going to be a partial truth at absolute best.

"The kind of misunderstanding where a guy in the mafia thinks I owe him several million dollars."

"Do you?"

"Technically. Maybe."

"Aslin," I say her name while taking a deep breath. "If you don't tell me exactly what's happening here this second, what happens next will make you wish the armed men from your mafia friend had taken you."

"Oh, I don't think that's possible," she grins. She's just so very pleased with her own cleverness. There's a certain madness about her, a self-congratulatory mood that makes it impossible for harsh reality to impinge now. "Luca would have them kill me, for sure. I have no doubt they'd shoot me in the head as soon as they found me. They don't want me alive. They can't really even risk taking the time to torture me."

"So your plan was to come here on vacation? And hope they didn't show up and murder you in front of us?"

"My plan was to stay a lot of places on vacation. I really do need to relax. My doctor said if I didn't find some way to calm down I was going to have a breakdown of some kind, ha!" She gives a little laugh, as if this is somehow funny. If I gave her the benefit of the doubt, I'd say she's nervous. If I didn't, I'd say she's absolutely mad.

"I need to hear all of this. Now. I mean everything."

"It's like I told you. I grew up in the country, single mom, no real options. I wanted to go to college, but I couldn't afford it, so I moved to the city. New York City, only city there is to move to. So I went and I found a way to afford it."

"What does that mean?"

"It means I met some men with money, and they gave me some money." She's being vague, but also incredibly specific with an economy of words. "The kind of men who wanted to do dirty things before they went home to their wives. The kind of men who needed to, you know. Anyway, one thing led to another, one guy led to another, I graduated, I got a job in one of their firms because I had an in with the boss, or rather the boss had an in with me." She glances up at our faces. "Anyway, uh, well, long story short, I stole the guy's money. A lot of his money. And then I ran the fuck away."

"Jesus fucking Christ," Jason swears.

"Don't worry," she says, lifting her hands again in that gesture. "I'll move on. I basically have to. This is way too close for comfort. They're on my tail and sooner or later, they'll circle back."

"What makes you think I'm going to let you leave?" I inter-ject. Aslin seems to think she's still a free agent, that my collar means nothing. I know that's because I haven't really spoken with her properly, but surely she understands something from context.

"Well, if you don't, you'll watch me get shot in the face. They're going to want to make an example of me. They're going to want to get my body and, you know... do things to it. I've seen what they do to their enemies before. It's not pretty. Sometimes they can't decide what mutilation they want to do and then they just do all of them. And you know what they call that? *The spaghetti.*"

A *slin*

They're going to kick me out of their camp now. They're not going to want this drama. I don't want this drama, and I am me.

"I'll get my things," I say. "Don't worry. I can hide nearby until the proper boat comes. I'm used to avoiding angry men."

"You're not going anywhere," Jason says. "Sit the fuck down."

I wasn't sitting down to begin with, and there's nowhere to really sit, but under his glower I find myself sinking down until I am sitting cross-legged on the jungle floor.

"Where's the money you took from this guy?"

"In accounts. Several of them. I split it up from Switzerland to Barbados. It's safe."

"Good, because it's going back."

"What? No! Do you know how hard it was to steal that money? That was supposed to keep me for the rest of my life. Never work again. I was going to go on this little trip, then buy a house somewhere remote. You know, one of those places that are practically nothing to buy, in one of those places where it costs practically nothing to live. And I was just going to be happily ever after on my own. And everything was going to be fine. I can't give that up."

"You can't keep it either. There are militia being sent to find you. And you're worried you're going to be killed and dismembered. That's not a happily ever after, Aslin."

"No? Well. It's not... there are worse endings."

I'm being defensive, but that's because nobody was ever supposed to know about this. It's a secret shame, or it was supposed to be.

"Listen, guys. I'm not worth this trouble. You should let me go. Right now, you're out of the loop. Nobody knows you ever saw me. But if you make me stick around, you're going to get sucked in, and then what? Then the men with guns won't ask questions. They'll kill you. Trust me, guys. It's been cute, but this is where it has to end."

They look at each other, and I'm sure they're coming to the same conclusion. I am a liability. I bring danger. I'm not just some brat who drinks too much and does what she wants and has an insatiable appetite for being dominated in bed. I'm the kind of trouble no man should ever engage with. That's what my ex said, right before I took his money, and he was right.

"Don't. Move." Jason growls the words down at me.

"Guys. Come on. I need to go. It's only a matter of time before they find someone who did see me, and then they'll be back. And then what? Then they find me. I have to go. Now."

S*oren*

There are tears in her eyes, though I don't think she knows that. She's trying so hard to be strong, to pretend that she's not absolutely terrified, but the way she hid, and how well she hid tells me she's scared. If those men had found her alone, she might have had reason to be.

"You're not going anywhere," I say. "Those men are out there, and you'd have to go past them to escape. There's only one way in and out of here. You'd be caught."

"I've gotten past men like that before. I don't know if you've worked this out, but me?" She points to herself with eye-shimmering pride. "More than meets the eye."

"Apparently," I agree.

"I'm getting out of here," she repeats.

"No. You're not."

This tension, this intensity, it's the hottest thing that's happened in a long time. I've missed meeting men with weapons. I've missed danger. Aslin is bringing something to our table that neither Jason or I have experienced in months, if not years: true adrenaline. She's exciting. She brings danger. This isn't healthy, but it is hot and I'm fucking hard.

I crouch down and take her chin between my thumb and forefinger. My grip is gentle, but firm. I want to let her know she's not going anywhere.

"Do you know what happens when bad little girls get caught stealing?"

"What?" Her question is breathy.

"They get made to give back what they stole and apologize."

"They really don't," she says defiantly. "It's mine. I took it, fair and square."

I kiss her. Deeply. Thoroughly. Yes, I know that I shouldn't be doing this. I should be getting to the bottom of what's going on, but there is no demanding anything from Aslin she doesn't want to give, and that includes information. She'll give her body before she gives her mind.

She kisses me back. I taste her need for forgiveness. Her body says so many things she can't. It tells me she doesn't want to go anywhere. It tells me she wants to be helped, maybe even to be saved.

I lay her back on the forest floor and I set about showing her that I am not going to be frightened away by a few grunts with their safeties on. She might be terrified of this Luca guy, but I'm not. I don't care who comes after her. She's mine to have. Mine to protect.

"The fuck?" Jason's question sounds distant. I'm sure he wanted to interrogate her, and demand to know what's going on. I'm sure he thinks we can sit her down and tell her what to do. I know better. I know her. I might not know any of the specific details, but I know her soul.

Aslin spreads her legs and lifts her hips to me. I free my cock and slide it over the dark and downy mound and then her softer slit. It feels as though we are constantly on the verge of losing her, either to her own recklessness, or to the consequences of her previous recklessness. She is a force of nature, a hot, wet, primitive piece of loveliness, and she's mine.

I feel an intense rush of pleasure as I sink inside her, kissing her passionately as I make love to her among the foliage.

"You're going to do as you're told," I tell her between kisses, my cock buried deep in her tight, clenching cunt.

"No, I'm not," she whispers back defiantly. Her eyes sparkle at me, enjoying this power play. This reaction is why she is so much trouble. Aslin loves conflict. Most people try to avoid it. It makes them feel sick and guilty and shamed. But it does something else for her. It makes her bright, and vital, and she shares that energy with the ones she is in conflict with.

"Yes, you are. That collar around your neck isn't just for show. I've claimed you. You're mine."

She laughs, but not in a mocking way. She laughs as though she knows something I don't. I cut that mirth short with a hard thrust that reminds her just who owns her pussy right now. With my cock stretching her cunt, there's no doubt as to who is in control.

Aslin lets out a very satisfying moan, and I feel her body soften beneath mine. This is what it takes to get her to submit. Hard sex and firm handling.

"You're going to regret this," she moans against my mouth.

She's wrong. No matter what comes next. No matter what happens, I will never regret being close to her. I love her. I feel a connection to her that has nothing to do with knowing the circumstances and facts of her life. I feel drawn to what is deep inside her. The part of her that calls to me, and the part whose call I cannot ignore.

10

J*ason*

Soren has fallen for Aslin. Hard. They're fucking with desperation, having the kind of sex that inevitably precedes separation. I am now officially fucking worried. Aslin is mixed up with the mafia, and Soren is obsessed with her. There's no walking away from what we've gotten ourselves into. We thought we were keeping her, but in the end, she's the one who has trapped us.

I listen to their mutual cries of orgasm, knowing that Soren is sinking himself into a mire he's not going to escape easily. Aslin is a sticky, dark, dangerous little thing. The worst part of this is that my cock is hard just listening to her. I want her as well. I need her as well. She has an addictive quality, a vulnerability combined with a relentless strength.

All I can do now is stay clear and try to maintain some kind of objectivity. We are no longer alone in the forest. Someone always has to stand guard. Tonight, that is me.

And a good thing too, for no sooner are they screaming their mutual orgasms than I hear a boat approaching quietly. The motor softly putts along toward us.

"SOREN!" I shout his name and go for the guns again. This time, they're already out and loaded. We are on alert.

Soren comes running, doing his pants up as he comes. His shirt is ripped. She's a wild fucking animal, our Aslin.

We meet the boat with weapons raised. The second visit is unlikely to be friendly. If they're back, it's because they've found out she's here. Any decent amount of inquiry would lead to that conclusion. Aslin was transported here by locals. They'll share that intel happily for a small fee. I am expecting an assault. The prow of the boat slides into view slowly, cutting little rivulets and ripples into the river.

"It's just me!" Barry calls out over the misty water. "Don't fucking shoot me."

"Barry?"

He's not lying. He is alone. He pulls the boat up to our little dock and gets out, hands raised. I lower my weapon. Soren never picked his up.

S oren

This isn't the kind of post-coital encounter I expected. I'm grateful to Jason for standing guard while I lost myself in Aslin. I didn't hear her fate coming up the river. I didn't sense the danger that has been wrapping itself around us slowly but surely since she arrived, an unseen anaconda of consequences.

"I came back to talk to you," Barry says. "I know she's here."

"How?" Jason grunts the question.

He nods toward the glittery plastic martini glass sitting up by the fire pit. "Either one of you going to tell me that's yours?"

"No."

"Doesn't matter," he says. "I don't give a shit about this. It's a domestic spat. We're not here to hurt her. We're here to take her back to her husband."

His words hit me like a charging elephant, knocking the air out of me.

"She's married?"

"She didn't tell you?" He shrugs. "Doesn't surprise me. From what I hear, she's a real piece of work."

Jason laughs. The sound isn't amused so much as it is the acknowledgement of what feels inevitable. Of course there's more to her story. Of course she hasn't told us what's important. Aslin doesn't tell anybody anything she thinks she doesn't have to. She keeps the world in the dark. She's terrified that someone else might have some kind of real knowledge of her.

"Aslin!" I call out to her. She is still nearby. She didn't run when she saw Barry. Maybe she knows him too. Or maybe she was listening earlier and knows he's not one of the people who plans to hurt her. Either one could be true. She's tidied herself up a little, pulled on new khaki pants, tucked her olive blouse into them. She's a neat little jungle explorer full of her own mysteries, but at least she meets my eye as I ask the obvious and inevitable question in the form of a statement.

"You didn't mention you were married."

"I'm not married. I mean, I am. Technically. I did marry Luca. I had to. I couldn't take his money if it wasn't also my money." She smiles at me, as if that should explain everything. And then she keeps talking, making matters exponentially worse. "You know what. I'm glad you know this. Because now you know I didn't actually do anything wrong."

She's absolutely conscienceless. When she tells me she's done nothing wrong, and I get the feeling she really believes that to be true.

"You ran out on your husband and slept with two other men," Jason says. His expression has become hard and closed. He's open minded, but not that open minded. Nobody likes a cheat. It's one thing to be shared between two of us, it's something else to choose to run out on a marriage.

"He forced me to marry him," she says. Jason and I exchange looks. We do this a lot around Aslin. We're checking in with one another because we can never quite be sure she's telling anything remotely close to the truth. Also, she just said that she had to marry him to get his money, and now she's claiming that he made her marry him. She's not coherent even within two of her own sentences.

"How can we believe that when every word out of your mouth is a lie?"

"I don't lie to you," she says, offended. "Sometimes I don't tell you everything right away, but let's be real, we've known each other like two weeks, and I didn't know I'd be tracked down. I was keeping you safe by keeping you in the dark. This was supposed to be a retreat. Not one big, long confessional. Yes, we had sex, but nobody asked anybody any questions. You could both be married for all I know. I figured what happens in the jungle, stays in the jungle."

She's right.

She's also wrong.

But really, ultimately, she's right. It's not like we're officially dating, and it's certainly not as though we've discussed anything to do with formalizing our relationship. We've all acted as though we're in our own personal Eden, as if nothing from the outside world would ever impinge on it.

It's not like she asked to be here, not after the first day, anyway. We've kept her here up until this point, with no knowledge of what's really going on with her. I've claimed her in my mind and my heart, but I have not gotten to know her yet, no matter how much I have tried.

"If you want to get this over with, take her back to Luca, and get his money back to him. Otherwise, we'll be heading out here at dawn and Big Dick will be grabbing her. I wanted to give you a heads up. Let you do the smart thing on your own," Barry says.

"No," Aslin says. "I'm not going back, and it's not his money anyway. It's mine. Possession is nine-tenths of the law."

There is a lot to wrap our heads around here. Aslin is married. Aslin is a thief. Aslin has to make amends to the man she seems to have either fallen victim to or conned. Regardless of the complexities, we have a mobster with a global reach about to send armed men in again. This has to be dealt with. Now.

"Thanks for the heads up, Barry," I say. There's enough tension in the air to indicate it's time for him to go. I'll make sure he's well compensated for saving our asses later.

"Good luck," he says in a tone that suggests we're going to need it.

I turn to Aslin, who of course looks the very picture of elegant moonlit defiance.

"You can decide to trust me, or you can decide to keep running. Either way, it sounds like your husband is coming for you. Do you want us by your side when that happens? Or do you want to be on your own?"

She twists her mouth one way, and then the other. "Well. When you put it that way, it feels like I should definitely have you with me."

"And we should do this in a location with actual police."

"I'm not so sure about that."

"Let me guess, you've got warrants," Jason sighs.

"I've got a lot of things," she says.

He practically snarls at her. I see the corners of her lips turn up. She enjoys making strong men angry. That's a pathology that must have gotten her hurt many times before. I am worried for Aslin. And I am beginning to be worried for us all.

"You lied to us, Aslin. You misled us. And in the beginning, that might have been reasonable, but it wasn't an hour ago. Not after armed men showed up here. You've put your life at risk, and ours along with it."

I see tears leap to her eyes. Is she sorry? Or is she just pissed off that she's been caught?

"Absolute psychopath," Jason growls.

"I'm not! Not even close! And no, I'm not telling you everything. I'm sorry about your lives and all, but I'm prepared to leave and go on my own. Nobody asked you to get attached to me. I was supposed to be here for a few weeks and then never see you again."

"Is that what you want? To use us as cover, then split?" Jason's accusation is harsh, but potentially accurate.

A *slin*

No. No, it's not what I want at all. I wish I could tell them the truth, but the truth is more dangerous than the lies, and it would only get in the way. I feel the same thing I've felt since I got here. Guilty. Guilty I dragged them into this, and even more guilty that I really don't want to leave them. I thought it would be easy to cut ties, but it's not. I'm attached to them, but I can't tell them everything. Not yet. Not unless I absolutely have to.

I've lived my life as a secret, never being able to trust anyone. People use information against you when they have it, and maybe Soren and Jason wouldn't, but they might. They might hate me or be disgusted by me. I can feel my web of lies collapsing around me, and it's freaking me the fuck out.

"I didn't factor you two into this plan," I say, telling them the truth. "I didn't think I would be found, and I thought if I was found, I'd be able to leave wherever I was. I'm sorry. This is way more fucked up than it should be. And yes, I have misled you. And I'm kind of still misleading you."

"So stop," Jason growls.

"Can't," I say. "I mean. Well, I can. But I won't. Should, maybe, but..."

"Enough, Aslin. If you won't tell us, we'll find out ourselves. But you know what? Making this harder on us is going to make it harder on you."

I draw in a deep breath.

"You don't want to tell us the whole truth?"

"No. I don't."

"Then you'll pay the price."

I should have known this would end over his knee. This is how it started, me being held over Soren's thighs, feeling a whole lot of intense emotions, wishing I was innocent, but knowing that I'm not.

They have to do something. They're mad. They're powerless. They have no idea who I am really. This is a temporary painful bandage for a problem neither one of us is able or prepared to resolve.

His big hand smooths over my ass. I feel a shiver of anticipation and fear. This isn't supposed to be hot. It's supposed to be serious.

"This is for lying to us. We won't abandon you, and I hope to god you work out that you can trust us soon, because this is dangerous and..."

"Just fucking spank her," Jason growls.

I'm glad I'm not over Jason's lap. He's really fucking angry; though, like Soren, he seems to still be on board with helping me. I don't know why they care. They have to have a hundred better things to do.

"You don't have to keep... you don't have to stand by me. I'm a mess. And I can't tell anyone anything. Ever. I'm always going to have secrets. It's just how I am."

Soren's palm lands on my ass. It's not as hard as I thought it was going to be. I thought he was going to be harsh as hell. The first time he put me over his knee, I freaked. I couldn't stand the intensity of his attention. This time isn't going to be any different.

"You can trust me," he says. "I know you don't believe that now, but I'm hoping if you hear it enough and see it enough, you'll start to believe it."

"Stop," I whimper. There are already tears in my eyes.

"I'm not going to stop. I'm not going to give up on you." He punctuates those promises with hard slaps that leave an intense sting. I feel like he's drumming them into me as even more slaps fall on my suddenly bared ass. He's pulled my pants down and is whipping his palm against my cheeks hard and fast. I've been punished before, but not like this.

They've given me whippings and spankings, but they've always been with a side of sex.

This isn't about sex at all. Soren is trying to make a point, trying to teach me something. I can feel how much he cares, and that scares the living fucking hell out of me. I don't know what to do with people who care about me. His arm snugs around my waist, and he hikes his knee up a little to present me at a better angle, and he just keeps spanking me, his palm meeting my ass time and time again, the heat and the sting and the ache growing with every single spank. I feel tears beading in the corners of my eyes, then sliding down my nose and dripping on the floor. I want to trust him, but I can't. I want to tell him the truth, but I won't. I'll take his discipline instead and let the pain absolve me of some of the ache in my chest.

S*oren*

She's not going to break. I knew that before I started. Getting through to Aslin is going to take time and commitment. I know Jason hates that, but he understands it too. Whatever she's hiding, it's deep and it's dark, and it's not going to pop out just because we ask nicely. It's going to be a hard-won battle. In the meantime, I'll turn her ass the right shade of pink as often as it takes to remind her that we are in charge, and we will always look after her.

I can see smears of my cum on her inner thighs as she kicks and squirms, reminding me I was inside her not that long ago. I made love to her thinking she was a naughty girl with a little secret. Turns out she's a naughty girl with a huge secret.

The squirming isn't because she's being a brat. She can't help it. A good, long spanking like this one invariably leaves a girl unable to hold herself still. I'd be lying if I said it's not satisfying to finally give her the thrashing she deserves.

"Soren!" She gasps my name and reaches her hand back in a helpless attempt to keep me from spanking her ass. I catch her open palm instead, and she snatches it away quickly. This is not going to be over anytime soon. This is going to be long. This is going to get through to her.

I give her a little break for a moment, smoothing my palm over her bright red ass. I can hear her sniffling, and I know she's probably crying, but what she's not doing is confessing.

"Is there anything you want to tell me?"

"No," she whimpers.

I start spanking her again, enjoying the way her ass bounces. She has a particular jiggle to her delicious little rear, a perfect roundness that I could smack all day and night long.

"That's a pity, because it means I'm going to have to keep spanking you."

"I'm not telling you anything!" She's getting defiant again.

"That's fine. You don't need to tell me anything. It's all going to come out in New York, isn't it."

"No! It's not! You don't need to come. You can just let me go!" She bursts into helpless tears. I don't know how much more she can take, and so I slow a little, and then a little more, until I'm holding her in place over my thighs.

"We're going to New York, little girl," I tell her as she sobs in my lap. "And we're going to make this all better."

11

A *slin*

Sitting on the tarmac at Kathmandu airport, waiting to depart, I am not a fucking happy camper. Soren has a superman complex. He thinks he can fix everything. He can't fix this. He shouldn't be trying. I think Jason agrees with me on that, but Jason's not talking to me. He's turned into a big male sulk.

This is not a trip I want to be taking. I planned to leave the US and never return. That was the whole point of the plan. Now I am being dragged back by the men who I half-trust, half-love, and maybe even half-loathe, though those percentages do not add up. I hate that I am being treated like an object, or a criminal; something for them to move about, a problem to be fixed. My reasons for doing what I did are still unknown to them besides the most superficial. They think I'm just a spoiled little monster with no sense. They think I'm something to be controlled. That's how men are.

I could tell them everything, explain myself, lay my history bare. But why should I? I do not owe anybody an explanation. Not even these two hunks of prime military beef. And knowledge is power. As a woman, it's the only power I have. I've learned to keep secrets over the years. A lot of them. Giving them up is not going to be easy.

They've put me between them. Soren has the window seat. I'm in the middle. Jason bookends me on the other side. We're going to be traveling for almost twenty-four straight hours, stopping in Dubai. Not really the place a wayward woman like me wants to make a dash for it. I think they chose that route on purpose. We could have connected through New Delhi, or Istanbul and London, or Paris. But all of those places represent an easy skip route. They booked through the one country where an unattended woman is going to have a hard time getting very far.

"Sit the fuck down," Jason snaps at me.

"I need to go to the bathroom."

"No," he growls.

"No? You want me to pee my pants?"

He's angry. I wonder if that's because he thinks I'm a cheater, or if it's because he just hates how much of an inconvenience I've become. He's been snippy and short since we packed up camp in the wee hours of the morning and sneaked through the village while Luca's little militia was still sleeping.

And here they are. The same group of mercenaries. I wonder how much Luca wasted on them. I guess it wasn't really a waste, though. He's getting what he wants. I'm coming back to New York, and he knows it.

"Oh! Hi boys!" I give a little finger wave as most of those men come filing onto the plane, boarding economy class. There aren't that many flights out of Nepal. Figures we'd all end up on the same one. Most of them ignore me. Big Dick gives me the kind of brutal stare that should scare me, but it just makes me laugh and flip him off. He's not a mercenary. He's one of Luca's men, and we've crossed paths before.

I've annoyed a lot of people over the last few months and years. I don't care. If they knew what I was doing, and why, they might feel sorry for me. And I don't need that. Sympathy from men is toxic. I'd rather they hated me than felt sorry for me. That's true even for Soren, who is the only person managing to keep the hard hate out of his eyes when he looks at me.

"Cut it out," Jason growls, pulling me back down into my seat. "You're spoiled to the point of sociopathy."

Seems like an overreaction, but whatever.

*J*ason

She's a brat. Worse than a brat. She's a married woman looking to fuck over her husband. There's nothing more dangerous on the planet than that. Scorned women are the kind of danger no guy should ever willingly encounter. Can't say I'm happy to be mixed up in this. Aslin's hot. She's the kind of crazy that sets the sheets on fire. But we should be walking away from this mess while we're still intact. Soren won't do that, and I won't abandon him. I owe him more than that. But I don't trust Aslin.

She'd tell me that it doesn't matter. She'd say she never asked me to trust her, and she doesn't trust me either. Everything about her is a frustrating mislead, and I think Soren and I are making a mistake by getting mixed up in it all.

I'm not here for her. I'm here because I owe Soren my life. He saved it more than once when we were at war, and vice versa. We trust each other with everything. There are no secrets between us. Ever. And here we are, traveling coach with the biggest bundle of secrets I've ever seen. We're heading into danger again, and I just have to trust that Soren and I will pull through like we've pulled through before.

12

S oren

"I'm going to tell you one last time," Aslin says. "This is a mistake. Let me go and tell Luca I got away. He'll believe you. I've gotten away from more security than the two of you before."

She has argued all the way from Kathmandu to this hotel in New York, a fact that has not put her in Jason's good graces. I am a little more understanding. She is scared, that much is obvious. I am hoping after today she won't have to be scared anymore.

"Quiet," Jason growls.

Jason's contact in Luca Vitori's camp has put us in touch with the man himself, which means we're about to get this situation resolved. With all going well, Aslin's going to be out of trouble, and we'll all be free to resume our lives without the prospect of militias hunting us down.

I plan to meet him in our hotel restaurant, a public place where a bloodbath would be an inconvenience to all concerned. It's in the part of Manhattan where an unofficial ceasefire exists among those with honor. The part where wives, children, and cars are safe from being riddled with bullets.

Jason is wearing a t-shirt and jeans. He refuses to wear anything tidier in case someone thinks he cares. It doesn't matter, he's staying behind the scenes. He elected himself to guard Aslin while I talk to Luca. I think that's a good plan. Someone needs to be with her at all times to stop her from getting hurt or being hurt.

Aslin has been surprisingly cooperative. She's given me account numbers and access codes for the money Luca says she stole. I'm going into this meeting being able to offer Luca what he wants, which gives me a good feeling.

I opted for a blue shirt, no tie, and charcoal dress pants. I look smart. Not mafia smart, but tidy enough to fit in downstairs where bankers and traders make the world go around.

"I will be back soon," I tell the disgruntled pair. "Try not to kill each other."

Neither one of them says very much as I leave. They're too busy giving each other looks that would kill if looks could kill. I sigh inwardly and hope that we can repair what's been broken by this series of lies. Saving Aslin has to be the priority.

I walk downstairs to the restaurant. Luca is already there. I see him the second I walk through the door. He's the sort of man that draws the eye, a kind of man who commands attention and respect. He's very handsome, and not as old one might expect. To hear Aslin, you'd think he was a creepy older man, the kind who would hit on a hot young woman and assume she was harmless because she was pretty. Luca looks young enough to know better, maybe mid-thirties, raven dark hair, brutal eyes, and the kind of expression that tells you he's comfortable with death. He is waiting for me in the restaurant, ostensibly alone, but I can see his men are everywhere, failing to relax in various poses, keeping a very close eye on me. My experiences in life have made me very sensitive to being watched. Right now, I am under intense observation.

"Hello," I say, offering my hand. "I am Soren Larsen."

"Luca," Luca says, offering his hand to shake. "Luca Vitori. I believe you have my wife."

Jason

"I need you to get out of my way, Jason," Aslin says.

I knew she'd try to pull some shit like this. The second Soren was gone, she was on my case to throw the plan out the window. She wants to run away. She doesn't trust us. She doesn't trust anyone. She needs to learn when she makes a deal with us, the deal means something.

"Not happening."

"I don't want to hurt you."

I laugh.

"Soren is down there, giving my money back to Luca. But that can't happen. And it won't happen. So there's no point standing guard. You don't want to keep me anyway, do you?

Not really. You haven't liked me since you found out I was married. You only fuck single ladies in the ass."

She's trying to get a rise out of me. She won't get it. She thinks I don't like her anymore, and she's wrong. Very wrong. I like her as much as I always have. The more trouble she turns out to be, the more I like her, and the less I like myself.

"Let me out, Jason." She scowls at me furiously, as if she can change my mind with the sheer force of her scared, spoiled will.

"No," I say. "Sit tight and let Soren handle this. It's all under control."

"Let me go now, Jason, or I'll make this hard for you."

I laugh at her threat. She's a little thing. A little thing who deserves to be spanked. Hard. And *still*, somehow. I don't know how many times we're going to punish her, or how many times it's not going to take. Soren says she's a long-term project. He's probably right.

Aslin's decided to make a stand. She's picked up a vase with some cheap flowers in it and looks at me. "Last chance, Jason. Get out of my way and let me go."

"Put that down, or I'll tear your little ass up."

The vase smashes against the wall, sending ceramic shards, water, and flowers everywhere. It's just the first victim in a series of inanimate objects that fall to our battle of wills. Aslin makes a dash for the door again, and again I block her. Frustrated, she retreats and grabs the little caddy of sugars and coffee. She throws those too, spilling pink, brown, blue and white packets all over the carpet.

"Stop that," I growl. "You're going to clean up this mess."

She responds by throwing an ashtray at a mirror. Both shatter, leaving sharp debris all over the carpet.

She's such a fucking brat, and Soren is not here to tell me to take it easy on her. If she's right, and this is the last time we're in the same room, I'm taking this last opportunity to teach her the lesson she needs to learn.

I grab her and toss her down on the bed. She's wearing a skirt, which helps access. I push it up over her ass. Her underwear is still in place. That'll come down later. I'm going to take my time with her. She wants to be dealt with, I'll deal with her.

Pinning her down on her back, I whip my belt out from my pants. It's awkward to hold a squirming woman down, but Aslin makes it slightly easier than it needs to be. She doesn't push up. She doesn't twist. She lies under me and puts up what I'm going to call the pretense of a fight. This girl loves being pinned down. She won't love what happens next. I loop the belt around my hand so the last several inches of the belt tongue are extended to just the right length.

I lift my hand and bring it down, testing the distance. I want to make sure I hit the right spot. With the way she's been behaving, she's due a proper punishment. One she won't forget. Soren wouldn't approve, but Soren's not here.

My belt lashes her pussy, the thick leather sweeping down against her sweet lips. She deserves this. This and so much more. She is a bad girl. She makes me want her. She makes me crave her. And she has Soren wrapped around her little finger to the extent we've flown halfway around the world to try to fix what she wanted to break all along.

She knows she deserves this. That's why she keeps her legs open. That's why her hips arch, and why her nipples are hard, why she relishes every painful stroke. She wants to hurt, but she doesn't want to stop misbehaving. She wants to play this game, over and over, time and time again. She wants to do bad things, and she wants to be hurt for them.

I see her spread for me. Her pussy is pink and dripping her essence. Her eyes are lidded, lashes curled up at me as she gives me that look, the one no man could ever resist.

As much as I want to stay away from her, I can't. My cock is fucking rock hard, demanding her. And she deserves to be fucked with a punished pussy. I want her to come on my cock with tears in her eyes. I want to make her come and I want to make her sorry at the same damn time.

I let her up and spin her around on the bed. Half the sheets come with her, but that doesn't matter, everything in this room is ruined, and a little more mess won't make any difference.

She looks up at me with those fuck-me eyes, and there's no resisting her. I have to have her. I pull my cock free of my pants and I plunge it inside her, thrusting deep inside her hot, tight, sore cunt. Her lips are so deliciously swollen and red, and her pussy is impossibly tight. She feels like heaven.

"You're fucking me while my husband is downstairs," she moans. "You think that marriage means something, but you're still fucking me."

She's a twisted, filthy little thing. She's corrupting me, and I am an equal and participating partner now. She's making me face who I am, and what I am. Not as honorable a creature as she wants me to be. Not as honorable a creature as I want to be. I am an animal, claiming my mate, driving my cock as deep inside her as possible, using her body and giving her mine.

"I don't give a fuck who you married. I don't give a fuck who says they have claim on you. You're ours. Mine and Soren's. And yeah, I'm going to keep you and whip your pussy as often as I need to, and fuck it too. You're mine, Aslin." I punctuate every word with a hard thrust. "You're. Fucking. Mine."

The bed makes a creaking, groaning sound. Through Aslin's moans and whimpers, I hear the unmistakable sounds of overburdened structure giving way. I can't stop fucking her. I won't stop fucking her. Being in between her spread thighs is the only thing keeping me sane right now. I keep hold of her, one hand in her soft, silky hair, the other gripping her throat. She arches her back up to me, her breasts jiggling with every harsh thrust as the bed slowly gives up beneath us and slumps down.

I ride her from the slanted mattress down onto the floor where the rug grips her butt with a lot more friction than the sheets did and stops her from sliding. With her finally in place beneath me, I grip her legs, hold them high, and pound into her, fucking her the way she needs to be fucked, and fucking her the way I have to fuck her.

She's beautiful. She's everything. She takes each and every one of my rough thrusts with feminine elegance, rolling her hips and gripping my cock with her inner walls. Even the lips of her pussy don't want to give me up, they hold onto me every time I pull out, and then her deep, tight insides welcome me again. I am falling into this woman. I am falling for this woman. I am the one holding her down and fucking her, but it still feels like she's the one in control somehow.

She screams as she comes. Her inner walls grip me, demanding I give her everything. Aslin always takes everything, and this time she'll take every drop. I growl, pumping my cum into her, pinning her down so she doesn't miss even a little bit. She's going to take every fucking drop of my seed. She's going to be filled up with my cream. My breathing is ragged as I hold my cock deep inside her and make sure she takes it deep in that bare little cunt.

Finally, when I've shot my load and her quivering cunt has stopped sucking every bit of my cum deep, I slide free of her. Or maybe that's wrong. My cock might be out of her, but I don't think I will ever be free of this girl.

~

"**W**hy did you say that?"

"What?" I'm still trying to get my breath back. Aslin is a workout and a half. I'm hoping that pounding settles her down for a couple of minutes at least, but as she sits up and looks at me with those dark eyes of hers, I realize I've tired myself out more than her by coming. Tactical error.

"Why did you say I'm yours?"

"Because you are."

She tilts her head at me.

"You don't want to be here. Soren dragged you here. You're a passenger, and things are going to get way more fucked up before they're done. So maybe it's not me who should be leaving now. Maybe it's you."

"Oh, fuck," I groan, rubbing my hands over my face. This is just unrelenting. "This is not the conversation I want to be having now."

"Do you just follow Soren around no matter what he does, is that it?"

"Yes," I say plainly. "That is it. But that's not all it is. I think you're a liar. I think you're dangerous. And I think you're still not telling us everything. I think my friend is down there risking his life because he loves you."

Aslin's features shift into a perfect expression of surprise. "He loves me?"

I stare at her. "You don't know that?"

"He never said it."

"We're here negotiating with a mob boss for you."

She shrugs. "Maybe that's part of the package deal, it's not like the rest of the vacation amounted to much."

"Yes, he loves you. I love you."

"What?"

"What?"

She says what first, I say what second. I am half-surprised I told her that. I'm half-surprised to find that it's actually true. I've fallen for her as hard as Soren has, it's just my better judgement tells me what a huge fucking mistake that is likely to be.

"You love me too? Why? God! Look at me."

"You're cute, and yeah, you're trouble, but you're, well, you're our kind of trouble," I admit.

"But I've lied to you... I'm still lying..."

"Yes. I know." I say it simply. "Would be really fucking nice if you'd knock that shit off."

"So you both love me," she says, her tone curious and a little strained. "And that's why you're here. Because you care about me?" She sounds so unsure, as if she's almost embarrassed to say it out loud.

"Yes, Aslin. That's why."

"Oh, man," she says. "Then there's some stuff I should really tell you."

13

oren

My meeting with Luca is going well. He's polite and patient. He could be cursing and threatening me, but I don't think Luca is the sort to make threats. I think he is the kind to carry them out, however. I am very well aware that if this does not go as well as he anticipates, or if I displease him somehow, death is a likely consequence. There seem to be even more of those quiet men dotted around the room, the ones who appear to be there for their own purposes, and yet don't do anything without reference to him.

"I understand Aslin took some money from you. I'd like to ensure the return of it."

"Very kind," Luca smiles with his lips, not his eyes. "Though I was going to ask for her as well. You do know, by now, that she is my wife."

"I would have thought it would be doing you a favor taking her off your hands. Or are you interested in remaining her husband? You keep threatening to have her killed, and yet it's obvious you don't want her dead."

Luca tilts his head at me with a handsome, composed smirk. It strikes me what a handsome couple they would make, Luca and Aslin. "Why assume that?"

"Because she's alive. And when men like you want someone dead, they tend to end up dead."

Luca takes that as a compliment. It's not.

"I want my money back, and you should be careful. She's bad news. Bad luck. She's a little monster."

He's said that twice now. Whatever Aslin did to him, besides steal an incredible amount of money, it has left a mark. The marriage, such as it is, is clearly not a happy one.

"If you two have any sense at all, you'll ditch her. She's a liability, and you'll never be able to trust her. I know she's cute, but she's like"—he makes a clawing motion with one of his finely manicured hands—"one of those deep sea fishes with the little light that hangs in front of the big needle-teethed face. She seems innocent and maybe even useful, but there's a big ugly void behind it, and you'll get sucked right in."

I sent Luca Vitori's name to Brian as well. I got his rap sheet and profile. I wanted to know exactly who I was meeting. He's a well-known figure in the criminal underworld. I know what this man is capable of, the crimes he's behind, the bodies he's left in his wake. He is not a man who scares easily, or who is given to meaningless dramatic outbursts. This is a man with a brutal past and more than likely, either jail or a violent death in his future, possibly both. Hearing him talk about the brat Jason and I fell for in Nepal this way is either amusing or concerning, depending how you look at it. She may be a little monster, but he is a bigger one. It is amusing that he should be horrified by her.

"I've organized a transfer out of her accounts, pending resolution into yours. We assume she spent some of it. If that's an issue, we can resolve it, though admittedly, not quickly. We can reimburse some of the..."

"Don't worry about it," he says, waving his hand. "If I get ninety cents back on the dollar, that's enough."

He's a businessman. Sharp. Smart. In another lifetime, we might have been friends.

"Thank you for being so reasonable. Give us the bank details and we'll get her out of your hair. Forever."

He cocks his head and looks at me curiously. "What are you two getting out of this, exactly? Because I'm telling you now, she's not what you think she is."

"We think she's a woman we can share, who we can take anywhere in the world with us and never be bored."

"Hm," he nods. "Maybe."

"I want something else," he adds.

"What's that?"

"A demonstration. I want to see you two handle her. I want to see what it takes to get Aslin to behave herself. And I want to be satisfied that when she leaves here, she's not coming back."

I think there's more to this story than meets the eye. I don't think he has any intention of hurting her. I don't think he ordered his mercenaries to hurt her, either. I think Luca has a thing for Aslin still. I can't blame him, she's that sort of girl. Addictive.

"She's going to apologize to you and make recompense. She has to learn that there are consequences."

"There aren't for Aslin. She never gets involved in anything without also having an exit strategy," he says. "I'd put money on her being gone from your hotel room before this meal is over."

"My associate has her. He's not an easy man to evade."

"Uh huh. You don't know her at all, do you," he laughs. "Tell you what. You get your money back to me, and you show me that you can handle her properly, and I'll let the matter drop."

"Let's go upstairs," I say. "Aslin is waiting."

This might be a mistake, but I want this matter finished and dealt with. It's obvious Aslin does not want to be married to Luca. If she did, she wouldn't have run away. She wants to be free. I want to make her free. She doesn't need his money. She has us.

Luca and I go up the elevator to the fourth floor. From the moment I open the door, I know I've made a mistake. The room is a mess. It looks like there's been a struggle, but I think we all know the struggle that took place here was no fight.

Aslin is tidying up on her hands and knees. She looks like she's been crying. On seeing Luca, she straightens immediately and rubs her eyes with her sleeve. It does nothing to make her look like less of a mess. We can smell sex and cum. We can see the rucked sheets and the smashed vases, and lamps, and broken paintings.

"Aslin," he says, a triumphant smirk passing over his features. We've delivered her to her personal devil. The second she sees him, she goes pale and wide-eyed. Even Jason looks concerned, and he has been lounging in the corner of the room in an armchair, watching her clean up until this point.

"Luca," she replies.

"I told you I would get you back," he says. "There's no escaping me, Aslin. There's nowhere on this planet you can go where I will not find you."

Aslin looks at me, and her eyes hold so much betrayal, even though we both knew this was coming. I think some small part of her thought I wasn't really going to go to him, and certainly not bring him back to her. I feel immediately guilty. I thought we were doing the right thing. I still think that, but I don't feel it. There's something wrong here. Something dark and twisted, something historical, maybe even ancient. I want to sweep her up and take her away, but I can't. Not yet. He needs his money. And I need him to renounce his claim on her.

"Luca," Jason says. He gets up and walks over, putting himself between Aslin and Luca. He sticks his hand out to shake Luca's hand. It's such a small gesture, that blocking motion, but it means a lot. As much as Jason doesn't want to admit it, he cares for her. Deeply. Maybe as deeply as me.

"Nice to meet you, Jason." Luca's response is smooth and calculated. "Thank you for *taking care* of my wife."

There's a suggestive lilt to those words that tells me he knows exactly what we've been doing with Aslin. It's unmissable. It perfumes the air, and it is written on all of our faces. If Luca is a jealous or possessive man, we might all die in this very room. Fortunately, Jason and I are accustomed to walking with death. I am not afraid, nor is he.

"I'm sorry I stole your money, Luca," Aslin says. "In my defense, you deserved it, I'm not sorry, and I'd do it again."

"This is what I'm fucking talking about," Luca sighs.

"What? You want me to lie?"

"I want you to act remotely sane, Aslin," I comment. Why can't she make this a little easier for us all? All she has to do is lie. She usually does that without issue. Why is it suddenly so difficult?

"Well. There's your first mistake," she smiles at me, and flickers a little wink. How is she suddenly composed? What game is she playing?

"She's not sorry, she's not going to be sorry," Luca says. "It doesn't matter what you do. She'll do whatever she wants to do. She doesn't have the part of the mind that makes her sorry. She's crazy."

Aslin

Luca is hot. He's always been hot. In another life, and in another time, we might have had a happy marriage. But that was never in the cards for us. I'm not cheating on him when

I sleep with Jason and Soren. He's not a real husband. And I'm not a real wife.

"Why don't you tell them the truth, Luca? Tell them who I really am. Now we're all here, seems the truth is inevitable now."

"You're Aslin Vitori," he says, predictable. "You're my wife."

"I was born Aslin Gato," I tell Jason and Soren. "I'm not a psychopath. And I'm not insane. I am the child of revenge. You married me to make a vendetta complete. You just never expected me to turn it on you."

"What are you talking about, Aslin?" Soren looks so confused, like a big, muscular, blond pup. I suppose I could have told him this earlier, but this is family business. It's a private vendetta that has been carried on for generations. It's not something I wanted to burden or taint him with. Soren and Jason were my perfect Adams in their remote Eden. They gave me peace. And then they brought me here. And now I have to tell them the things I never wanted them to know. And that pisses me off, because I know that things will never be the same after this confession. This isn't like pushing Jason into a lake or getting lost on mountain. This is a legacy of blood and death going back generations.

"Remember I told you my mother raised me alone in the countryside? Her name was Victoria Gato. Her father and my father were murdered by Vito Vitori. Vito, if you don't know, is Luca's father."

"Oh. Shit." Jason curses.

"You starting to see how this all works? What Luca has was stolen from my family. He took everything. All I did was take some of it back. But then you two had to intervene, with your morals and your righteousness. You had to know better than I did, even though you knew nothing at all." I sound a little mad at them. I am mad at them. I know I lied, but I had every right to lie. What I was doing, I was doing to avenge my family. I didn't plan to bring them into it. In the end, they didn't give me a choice.

"You could have told us..."

"It wasn't your fucking business!" I turn to face both of them. All of them. Jason with his serious, yet crestfallen expression. Soren, who finally looks concerned the way he should be. And Luca, who never stops looking smug. "I was trying to get away. I told you that a hundred times. But you wouldn't let me. As soon as this asshole sent his goons, you knew better. So. Here we are, with an entitled little rich boy who thinks he owns me. Oh, and nobody is cheating. The marriage was never consummated."

"Only because you ripped me off and ran off between the wedding and the wedding night," Luca says. "You would have loved being my wife, Aslin. I know how to be rough too."

"Alright," Jason says. "Give him the money, give her a divorce, and let's call this a day. We're done here."

"I don't know if we are," Luca says.

"He's not going to let me go," I sigh. "You've brought me back, and now he's going to take me for his own."

Luca's expression turns shark-like. "Aslin is right, I'm afraid. She'll be coming with me. My ancestors did take everything, and they'd be very upset with me if I let her go. Thank you for returning her, boys. I can assure you that you will be well compensated. A million dollars each should make up for your lost time."

I knew Luca would try to keep me. And I knew he'd try to pay Soren and Jason off. He thinks money solves all problems. He thinks money is all anybody cares about. He's wrong about the rest of the world, but he is right about himself. He's predictable. And because he's predictable, he's easy to beat.

"Wait," Soren says. "That's a very generous offer, but..."

"I don't want this to get bloody," Luca says. "I thank you for your service. To your country, and to me, of course."

"Aslin can choose where she goes," Soren says.

Does he know how much he sounds like an after-school special? Does he know how much he looks like one right now? That button-down shirt is so cute. It makes him seem much less dangerous than he is. When I see him, I see the sweaty jungle man who swept me off my feet. I know the muscles that hide beneath that plain fabric. God. I really want to get that shirt off. I swing between anger at these men and desire for them so fucking quickly. It's like sexual whiplash.

"Of course she can't," Luca laughs at him. "She didn't choose to come here, did she? You brought her here because it was the right thing to do. You saw how wild and untamed she was, how badly she needs a firm hand. She's not safe on her own. Not for herself, or for anyone. So now I will take her home, where she will learn to be a good and dutiful bride. We will consummate our marriage, and she will learn to obey. You two have taught her a great deal in a short time, and thanks to you, she now knows there truly is no escaping me."

"I am really sorry, Luca," Soren says.

"Don't be sorry, be..." Luca never gets to finish that sentence, as Soren grabs him and puts him in a chokehold. It is the most satisfying thing I have ever seen, Luca Vitori squirming in another man's arms like a moth with its wings trapped. He has no idea how to break the hold, and though he tries a few desperate kicks and elbows, they do nothing to Soren who is used to taking damage.

Luca's boys are all downstairs. He's alone up here. He doesn't want anybody to know what I've been doing, or who I have been doing it with. He wanted to take me home and pretend the last couple months never happened. And now, because of that pride, Luca is vulnerable in Soren's arms, not because he's weak, or small, but because Soren has spent a lifetime practicing the art of subduing those who do not want to be subdued, and Luca has never been in a fight he hadn't already won.

Soren has him out like a light in under a minute. He eases Luca's insensate body down to the ground and kneels beside him, checking his pulse. What a gentleman. I just finished getting laid, and yet here I am being turned on all over again. There's just something sexy as hell about someone who does a whole lot of damage and then follows it up with tender loving care.

"Alright," Soren says, slipping a small zip up case out of his pocket. It looks like what a tidy junkie might use to store a handy dose of something fun. But of course, it's not. It's a sedative, and he brought it with Luca in mind. He has everything all ready, including the tourniquet. I'm starting to wonder if there's more about Soren I don't know. Did he used to use? Is he a nurse in his spare time? How long has he been carrying around a sedative?

Soren flicks the tip of the needle before putting it neatly into a vein. Luca doesn't feel it. Doesn't even flinch while unconscious. We could do anything to him. We could get the kind of revenge my family has only dreamed of.

"That'll give us an hour," he says. "Plane is half an hour away on the runway, gassed and ready to go."

"What?"

"Let's go, Aslin."

Soren says the words firmly. I don't know if I'm being rescued or kidnapped at this point. I do know that I'm curious.

"You should have told us about the history between your family and his," Soren says reproachfully as he ushers me out the freight elevator. Obviously, we're taking the surreptitious way out of the building. "It would have made your story a lot more sympathetic."

"I didn't know that you'd care. Besides, I did marry him. He thought he was forcing me into marriage, but I was letting him make me. I wanted access to his accounts, and I got it. I'm not the good girl in this story, and I'm no victim."

14

S*oren*

Aslin is definitely no damsel in distress. She's a wicked, vengeful, sweet, disastrous little minx, and like I told her when I put the collar on her the very first time: she's mine.

Her marriage to Luca does nothing to change that. If the man hasn't gotten an annulment, given the marriage was never consummated, then I have to wonder if he's not also obsessed with her. There's something about Aslin, an addictive quality. Once you get a taste of her, she's almost impossible to forget.

Jason nudges me on our way to the airport. "Just to recap, we're running off with the wife of another man, a mob boss, and we've got millions of dollars of his money in anonymously numbered accounts," he says.

"I know."

"I'm fucking loving this," he grins. "This is going to be a hell of an adventure."

"Luca might try to kill all of us," Aslin adds. "He won't take that lightly."

"Maybe," Jason says. "I don't think so. I think he's going to come for you, though. I think this is going to be an international game of high stakes keep-away that we enjoy while we spend his money."

"You two have really mellowed on... well, a lot of things," Aslin observes. "Look how much I've corrupted you. Or maybe I didn't. Maybe you were just as bored sitting out there in that jungle with your legs crossed as I was."

"Where do you think we're going, Aslin?" I ask her the question gently.

"I don't know? Somewhere with a pool."

"No, sweetheart. We're going to another remote location, and you're going to get the treatment we promised you. Ninety days of meditation, relaxation, and obedience."

"No!" She lets out a gasped moan. "Anything but that. A thousand lashings rather than sitting still. I think I hate that more than anything. I think I might even go back and wake Luca up rather than do that."

"Such a fuckin' brat," Jason laughs.

We've arrived at the private airport, where our plane is humming happily on the tarmac. It starts spinning its rotors as we approach, looking almost excited to sweep us away to fresh adventure.

We are not quite outside the law — there's nothing that says two gentlemen cannot accompany a technically married woman on her travels, but we are definitely outside the moral code employed by the mafia, of that I am certain. The law may not be coming for us, but I am certain Luca will. Some might say we were stupid for not killing him, but we know all too well that killing someone has wider consequences than the immediate death. It might seem like a convenience, but it usually leads to endless bloodshed. Best case scenario, Luca gives up and moves on. Worst case, well. We'll get to that when the time comes.

I sweep Aslin up into my arms and carry her up the stairs to the plane. It's romantic, but it's also my way of making sure she gets where I want her to go. I wouldn't say I trust Aslin. Not as far as I can throw her. But I do love her. And she is mine.

EPILOGUE

slin

Another day, another jungle, another early start. I sit quietly, Jason to my left, and Soren to my right. We are meditating. Well, they are. I'm thinking about the expression on Luca's face when Soren was choking him out. He was looking me dead in the eye, and he'd never looked so surprised. I've been replaying that over and over since we left. It's the most satisfying thing I have ever seen. It might be the most satisfying thing I ever see.

"Quit giggling, brat," Jason nudges me.

"Stop trying to make me be all peaceful and calm," I nudge back. "You know I don't go for this shit."

"And you know we told you we'd give you what you signed up for. A strict meditation retreat."

"We're still pretending to do that?"

"We were never pretending," Soren says, without opening his eyes. "Quiet."

He's sterner than he was before. He thinks if he doesn't let me get away with anything now, I'll somehow be less of a liability. I think it's cute, and if it makes him feel any better I'll let him keep his illusion of control. That's half the reason I'm sitting here now, to throw these poor guys a bone. To let them think they're making some headway with me. Everybody needs a little hope in their lives.

"Cut that out," Jason growls at me.

"What?"

"I can feel you smirking."

"You cannot."

He opens one eye at me. I'm not smirking. I'm grinning.

"Brat," he declares, reaching for me to try to pull me over his knee. I'm quicker than him. I scramble away just as his hand closes around my wrist. Or maybe he lets me go at the last moment. Either way, I dash up toward the tents we're living in, and he gives chase. Jason could easily catch me if he wanted. He's playing with me. Letting me win, or at least feel like I might win. Kind of like what we did to Luca, except I'm not waking up like a chump.

"The two of you get back here now," Soren says. He's still sitting there cross-legged. Nobody is getting any meditation here. There's no inner peace. There's chaos, and fun. And freedom. Yes, I'm free, maybe for the first time, if freedom means being known for what you are, or at least, a part of what you are.

"Alright," Jason says, catching me again and dragging me back. "Take this seriously."

I have lived my life as a refugee, hiding from the powerful mafia family that has always been at war with mine. I'm the very last of our blood, and their last chance to dominate our bloodline completely. I'm just trying to make my way in the world, all the while knowing that will never be allowed. Luca saw me as the final piece in the puzzle, one last conquest to forever humiliate my family. Fucking me, making me have his baby, that would have given him everything his ancestors dreamed of. I've denied him that triumph, and I've bloodied his nose, twice. It doesn't go anywhere toward truly making up for everything my family lost, but it's a small strike back. If he's not smart enough to leave me alone, it won't be the last strike.

Technically, we are now on the run, but I don't feel it. I feel content and at peace with my two lovers. Soren and Jason are different but perfect in their own ways. Each of them gives me something I need, and hopefully I give each of them what they need in turn. I'm still stunned they fell in love with me. Not just lust, but love. I know it's real because they're still not tired of me. They're there every morning when I wake up, and I fall asleep in their arms each and every night. They give me safety, security, and a place to be — between them.

Jason sets me down in the middle again, and we settle. The birds sing. The frogs croak. The world spins. And I win.